Praise for 'Sunset Trip'

"Take the expressway to your skull as Ben Vendetta delivers another lysergic slab of subcultural mayhem, oozing with unabashed style and pizazz in *Sunset Trip*! A tale told thru the rhythm, chronicling life in the peripheries of endearing veteran indie rocker geek, Drew. Set amidst the fallout years of the shoegaze scene (psychedelia's last gasp) as the original indie epoch bids farewell to the 20th century in a cataclysmic cloud of hedonistic chaos! Will Drew get out alive, or end up behind the cemetery gates pushing up psycho daisies? Vendetta's magnum opus is realised from the inside looking out, depicting a world now far from view, though still 'too real to feel'."
— Sam Knee, author of *A Scene In Between*.

"A tale of outsiders brought together by rock 'n' roll and the anxiety of missing your chance in life."
— Jim Reid (The Jesus and Mary Chain)

Praise for Ben Vendetta's work.

"A blast from the post-punk past that brings back mid-eighties Britain in one wired, synaptic rush, a coming-of-age story that is as poignant, political, hormonal and hilarious as the sounds it celebrates."
— Cathi Unsworth, author of *Weirdo, Bad Penny Blues, The Singer*.

"It's an addictive read, an affirmative and faithful story of sex, drugs and rock & roll. Where an equivalent

novel such as Nick Hornby's *High Fidelity* becomes ever more unrealistic to get to its happy ending, *Wivenhoe Park* retains a believable optimism through sheer faith in rock & roll."
— Paul Rayson, *Muso's Guide.*

"I enjoyed *Wivenhoe Park* thoroughly. Ben Vendetta captures the youth feel and mood of those times quite vividly."
— Sam Knee, author of *A Scene In Between.*

"This is classic coming-of-age stuff. Drew makes friends, hangs out with bands, dates inappropriate girls, takes drugs and a whole lot more. But what makes *Wivenhoe Park* such a joy is that Ben writes in a very engaging way... If you ever enjoyed *High Fidelity*, went to a British university in the mid-'80s or are counting the days until Cherry Red reissues the legendary C86 compilation, you'll love this."
— PopJunkie

"Vendetta brings back an '80s era when a stunning, now-legendary post-punk/indie rock scene was blazing in Britain, yet this time, unlike with punk rock, a smaller slice of Americans followed its brilliance. He slyly evokes this in a coming-of-college-age story of throwing off the influence (and snares) of normal Middle American life by instead immersing himself into the thick of the NME/Melody Maker/Sounds-fed maelstrom in England itself."
— Jack Rabid, *The Big Takeover.*

"If John Hughes were still alive... well... he'd never touch this story. It's too full of the sort of gritty realism

that never made it into his well-scrubbed coming-of-age stories."
— Robert Cherry (former Editor-in-Chief, *Alternative Press*)

"For those of us who came of age in the '80s and didn't give a hoot about bands like Foreigner or Poison but instead wanted REAL music then *Wivenhoe Park* will be a real page turner that's hard to put down. It certainly was for me."
— Tim Hinely, *Dagger.*

"*Wivenhoe Park* wrenched me back to a mid-'80s Britain where punk was dead and alternative/goth ruled. If birds, booze and Bunnymen are your thing, as they are mine, then dust off your Sisters of Mercy LPs, squeeze into your Meat Is Murder T-shirt and enjoy the ride."
— Dave Hawes (*Catherine Wheel*)

"Ben Vendetta takes you back to a simpler time when culture and relationships were complicated but fun, and when music really mattered to your life. This dive into historical fiction is like a post-punk version of *High Fidelity*, with a bit more grit, sass, and reality. It's a great read."
— Tony Schinella (Award-winning journalist, broadcaster; musician)

"Vendetta's strengths as a writer don't just include an encyclopedic knowledge of '80s and '90s UK indie/shoegaze/Britpop, but also an ability to cultivate sentences and paragraphs that make it almost

impossible to put this book down."
— Matthew Berlyant, *The Big Takeover*

"Vendetta is obviously a serious indie fan and, in amidst all the Blur, Oasis and Verve references, the pages of this enjoyably witty and fast paced novel are littered with the names of relatively obscure bands that you've probably forgotten – Lush, Auteurs, Ultra Vivid Scene, cast, etc. Immediately after finishing *Heartworm*, this reviewer spent several hours revisiting the '90s on YouTube."
— Olaf Tyaransen, *Hot Press*

"*Heartworm* will make you nostalgic for the mid-1990s Brit-rock scene – even if you never lived through the era. But this is no moody walk down memory lane. The second book in Vendetta's trilogy about rock journalist Drew is a moving and often very funny look at growing older, sometimes not so gracefully, as the post-college years turn into adulthood. And, it comes with a great soundtrack, from the Jesus and Mary Chain to Oasis to Whipping Boy."
— Laura DeMarco, *The Plain Dealer*

Sunset Trip

Ben Vendetta

Ben Vendetta is the author of the novels *Wivenhoe Park* (2013) and *Heartworm* (2015). He has an extensive background in the music industry as a writer, magazine publisher, and PR Director, and is the co-founder of independent label Elephant Stone Records. Vendetta lives and works in Cleveland, Ohio.

For George Nemeth
(1968 - 2016)

and

Christopher Tucker
(1971 - 2008)

All Farewells Should Be Sudden

I often fantasize that I'm Richard Ashcroft in the *Bittersweet Symphony* video, but today the thought of pushing pedestrians out of my way doesn't enter my mind as I begin the short journey from the Boston Common T Station to my office in the Financial District. Mark Jennings is in town. I haven't seen him since rehab and I'm anxious about our reunion tonight.

The Common was my favorite spot in the city before I became an investor relations hack. It's a lovely green space with a large pond, reminiscent of St. Stephen's Green in Dublin, where I used to live, but these days the scenic walk to work only saddens me. I can barely muster the energy to focus on the pavement in front of me. I bum a cigarette from a well-dressed man who's smoking outside my building. He probably hates his job as much as I hate mine, judging by the fact that he's pale, angry and overweight. I'm running late, but I need a little something extra to take the edge off.

My boss Fran is pacing in front of my desk when I arrive at the office. She isn't much older than me, barely forty, but you'd think she was pushing sixty with her frumpy mannerisms and fashion sense. My co-worker Brent once joked that she probably masturbates to the L.L. Bean catalog. Fran pounces on me before I have a chance to adjust my eyes to the glaring fluorescent light and taupe walls, which seem better suited for an insane asylum.

"Where the hell have you been, Drew? I need you working on that earnings report. We're issuing it today after market close."

"It's almost finished, Fran. Just a few more edits."

"I need it on my desk in an hour. No more excuses."

As she storms off, I log on to my PC and open the file, trying to focus, but I can't concentrate. I keep thinking about Lou Reed. Mark and I would listen to *Transformer* during downtime in rehab. We'd take a boom-box out on a patio with spectacular Pacific Ocean views and soak in the vibes. Lou looked so strung out on the CD cover, yet confident and smug, as if he were egging us on to join him for another perfect day. In retrospect, an odd listening choice for two addicts.

Brent shoots me a quick email, asking what's up with Fran.

- Is she on the rag? She seems bitchier than usual.

- She's always like that, I respond. *- She's a fucking cunt.*

I leave my desk, ignoring the evil eyes of hyper-enthusiastic colleagues imprisoned in cluttered cubicles, chock full of family photos and clichéd motivational quotes, and make my way to the rest room. The report is nowhere near complete; I'm stressed enough that I'm tempted to jerk off in one of the stalls. Despite being in the rat race for the past two years, part of me still identifies as the 'almost famous' rock critic who contributed to magazines like *Spin* and *Alternative Press*, glamorizing the lifestyle I wrote about, until it crashed down in a sea of drugs and heartbreak.

Has it really been three years since I wrote my best piece; a lengthy feature on the Dublin band Whipping Boy? I maxed out a credit card and flew to London to conduct the interview and witness their gig at the Shepard's Bush Empire. That's how much I bled for the cause in '96. Whipping Boy supported Lou Reed that evening, and I was lucky enough to meet the legend, a true gent. What would Lou think if he saw me wasting away in office purgatory? What would Mark say? He begged me to keep the rock 'n' roll dream alive.

"Take it easy, man," he said. "Do something chill, like work at a used record store. Office jobs are bullshit. Dudes like us need to create. We may be here to detox, but the real secret is to *retox* on rock 'n' roll. That's the purest feeling you'll ever know. I'm not into God or the twelve steps or any of that bullshit, but music is real. I'm out of here tomorrow, man, and I'm never coming back. It's been too long since I've played in a band and made records. Booze and cocaine have held me hostage for far too long. I want to live again. Don't you, Drew?"

"I don't know. No offense, but I'm not drinking the Kool-Aid this place is selling. I've disappointed everyone I've ever loved, and I'm having a hard time dealing with that."

"Give it time, man. You have another month in this joint to get your shit together. If you're stuck when you get out, you can count on me."

I gaze into the mirror, wishing I could destroy the man staring back at me. I know I look good in my black suit, crisp white shirt, and black tie – a reservoir dog in the corporate world – but I feel dead inside. My hair is long in front but cut far too conservatively for my liking on the back and sides. I've morphed into an old acquaintance I used to get wasted with, an ex-rock 'n' roller turned jaded investment banker. For the first time in years, my family is proud of me but I know I'm a fraud, a ticking time-bomb waiting to detonate. How did that The The song go, *This Is The Day*? The one where he's haunted by painful memories? Because mine are crippling me, taking me to dark, suicidal places.

Emily is still on my mind. We split up last year, but she still keeps tabs on me, probably out of fear that I'll do something destructive again. Whenever I see her, my heart aches with regret. The right girl at the wrong time; a story as old as dirt.

We met three years ago when I moved from Dublin to Boston to house-sit for my brother Paul, a Harvard professor, who had just begun a sabbatical at Stanford. I was thirty-one, broke, and separated from my now ex-wife Claire, who had left me to start a commune in England with a self-proclaimed shamanic crystal healer. Emily was twenty-two and full of vigor, a cute Winona Ryder lookalike about to graduate from Harvard and conquer the world. It worked for a while until Emily abruptly broke things off to take a job in San Francisco and rekindle with an old flame.

She returned to Boston at the end of the year when her relationship took an ugly, violent turn. We started again, both of us in the emotional gutter. Me, scarred from my freshly-finalized divorce; Emily bruised from her ex-lover's punches. We moved into an apartment in the trendy Davis Square neighborhood. Emily started writing for the local entertainment rag *The Boston Phoenix*, and I landed an under-achieving desk job at Harvard. To outsiders, we were a good fit. A nice-looking rock 'n' roll couple making the scene.

We went to concerts three or four nights a week at favorite haunts like the Middle East, TT's, and the Paradise. Sometimes, I would get jealous that Emily was the one documenting it all. I stopped writing for *Spin* in '96 after falling out with my boss and, despite offers from other magazines, I convinced myself that I was a relic; that my ship had sailed. Rock 'n' roll is a young man's game, I told myself as I suppressed the creative urges with drink and drugs, but even heavy intoxication couldn't stop the night terrors.

The dreams ran the gamut from standard monster fare to vivid recollections of Claire's second suicide attempt, one I experienced firsthand at her father's home in Belfast. This occurred in the autumn of '96, after our divorce should have been finalized. I was unable to track down Claire to get the papers signed, so I contacted her father and learned that she had returned to Belfast. He told me that Claire had turned up at his doorstep with no warning, malnourished and in a disheveled mental state. He said that Claire was barely eating and speaking, that she was fearful her ex-lover would track her down and harm her. Her father sought out medical attention, but it wasn't enough. A few days later, Claire nearly overdosed on sleeping pills.

I flew to Belfast and tried to help, but Claire was a shell of her former self. It was evident that it would take years of therapy to undo the damage. One evening, I was jolted from my sleep by loud screams. I found Claire in the bathroom, her arm bleeding profusely from razor cuts, her white nightdress splattered in blood. Claire's therapist thought my presence would hinder her recovery so I left Belfast, broken and guilt-ridden, and returned to Boston. Paul, who had recently returned from Stanford, graciously bailed me out for a second time.

A shrink put me on heavy-duty meds, but even those couldn't exorcise the nightly reminders that I hadn't done enough to save Claire. One night, while Emily was out, I washed down a fistful of pills with a large glass of whiskey. I laid down on the floor, my head spinning out of control, wondering what would happen next. I was half-scared that I had done something stupid, and half-excited that whatever happened next couldn't be worse.

Everything went white. I found myself alone in a vast, bright room without a soul in sight. It felt like I was in a lucid dream – I knew who I was – but something was different, more permanent. Nothing mattered. The heartache was gone and though I was alone in limbo, I wasn't fazed. I was at one with my surroundings and didn't want to leave.

I came to on a hospital gurney, surrounded by Emily and several paramedics. There was bloody vomit on my T-shirt and I kept dry heaving as I tried to find my voice.

"What's your name?" asked one of the medics.

"Drew," I gasped.

"Do you know where you are?"

"In my apartment."

"What year is it?" asked medic number two.

"1997."

"Looks like you're going to be okay, Drew," said medic number one, "but we need to take you to the hospital for tests. You can thank your girlfriend for saving your life. She gave you CPR and induced you to vomit. If it had been much longer, you could have choked and died."

"Like Jimi Hendrix?"

No one laughed (though I swear one of the medics suppressed a smile). Emily started to cry, and I felt like shit.

I spent a week at Mount Auburn Hospital, where they tried to scare me straight with a list of newly-discovered ailments. I was told that my liver was so fucked up that if I continued to drink I could do myself irreparable harm. I also learned I had a heart murmur.

When I got out of rehab, I thought my life would take a turn for the better. The Kool-Aid worked for a while. I moved back to my parents' house in Michigan to embrace Mark's retox philosophy. I talked to Emily every day, but she seemed distant. My near-death experience fucked with her mind. Me, halfway across the country in a heavily medicated state wasn't helping matters. As the months passed, I knew it was time to start looking for a job, to find something to live for. I had mixed feelings about returning to Boston. I missed Emily but felt like I needed a fresh start. I was scared that if I moved back east I would fall into old habits. I was about to start a job at a used record store in Ann

Arbor when Paul gave me a lead on an investor relations gig at an international bank in Boston. He had a friend who worked there and said that the job would be cake; editing press releases, personnel announcements, that kind of thing. Great pay but nothing too stressful, he said.

Within weeks, I regretted my decision. Despite the promise of an easy gig, twelve-hour days became the norm and the constant deadlines were giving me ulcers. The rigid dress code at work didn't help matters. I felt like an absolute tool. A friend of Emily's joked that I looked like David Byrne in Dockers when I met them for dinner after work on a dress down Friday. I should have quit but a masochistic sense of pride took over. Time to force myself into adulthood, even if it kills me.

Emily and I rarely saw each other. We agreed to take a break while I got my act together. She told me she was going to move out when our lease ended. I begged her to reconsider, that I still loved her, but she said that I needed to learn how to love myself first. Typical chick stuff, but she was right.

I'd come home from work at ten or eleven in the evening and she'd be out with friends at gigs, galleries, or restaurants, living her life to the fullest, while I delved deeper within. I bought a bottle of whiskey with the pretense that I'd take a single shot every night; a small reward for getting through another day. One shot quickly escalated into half a bottle and it didn't take long for Emily to cotton on.

Emily was crying uncontrollably the day she found out. She told me how I saved her life, how it broke her heart that she couldn't return the favor.

"You're an addict and you're going to kill yourself," she said. "I can't watch you die."

She moved out the next day. Virtually everything belonged to her. Overnight, our hip modernist pad, full of vintage furniture and collectibles, morphed into a lonely vampire's lair.

*

Our HR guy John is waiting for me when I return. Normally he's quite mellow – he has a beard, which is downright rebellious at a financial institution – but, right now, he looks pissed as fuck.

"Drew, I need to speak to you immediately."

I follow John to his office. When I step inside, he slams the door and I suppress a smile, remembering his email signature, which says: *My door is always open.*

"Do you know why you're here?" he asks.

"I have no idea."

John hands me a print out of my email exchange with Brent, noting that I copied Fran in my response. My hands are shaking, and I feel sick to the stomach.

"This is unacceptable, Drew. As of this moment, you are no longer employed here. Do you have anything to say for yourself?"

"No," I say. "All farewells should be sudden."

Funny Cigarettes

When I get home, I pop a Valium – I'm allowed one pill every eight hours – and take a few deep breaths. I've become a heavily medicated robot, barely going through the motions. For a guy who just got fired, I'm surprisingly apathetic.

The apartment is empty and soulless. Several CD shelves and a half-dozen crates of records line the living room wall, but not much else. Mark once told me that rock 'n' roll saves lives and sometimes it feels like music is my only friend, the only thing keeping me afloat in my foggy, dreamlike world. I put on an old Jesus and Mary Chain record. William Reid announces that he's going to the darklands. I'm already there, waiting to greet him.

I make a peanut butter and jelly sandwich but have no appetite, barely finishing half of it. Mark's probably at the Middle East by now, getting ready for sound-check. I decide to surprise him at the club. I change into a pair of jeans, black T-shirt, Chelsea boots, and a black leather jacket, realizing that I'm probably dressed exactly like he is. Though our paths only crossed for a week in rehab, it felt like we were separated at birth.

On my first day, literally an hour after I checked in, one of the counselors told me about Mark. She thought the two of us would bond when she found out I was a music guy. The joint I was staying at was big on the buddy system.

"Mark's a musician," she said. "I think you'll get along."

I said nothing, figuring he was going to be an ex-hair metal hack like Brett Michaels. When she escorted me to the common room I experienced an embarrassing fanboy moment.

"Fuck, you're Mark Jennings," I said.

Mark smiled. I could tell he was pleased that I knew who he was. He was thinner than I remembered when I saw Solarstar in '87. He was dressed entirely in black, save for a pair of leopard print boots, still rocking that immaculately messy haircut (more Bunnymen than The Cure) that all the goth girls loved. Stylish as he was that day, he looked ghostly pale, like he was knocking on heaven's door. The only thing that betrayed Mark's quintessential English rock star looks was his nasally Midwestern accent. He was the sole American in a British buzz band.

"So, you're a Solarstar fan?" Mark asked after removing his shades.

"Fuck yeah! I saw you at Whelan's in Dublin. I interviewed you and Matthew St. James for *Hot Press* before the gig. You probably wouldn't remember. I'm sure all those interviews became a blur."

"They did, especially toward the end. I did most of the talking because Matthew was so strung out. He used to sit on a stool and stare off into space when we played live."

"He did the night I saw you, but I'm sure you're sick of guys like me dredging up the past."

"No worries, man. Despite how it went down, those three years in Solarstar were the best. Nostalgia is a bitch. Kicking drugs is cake compared to killing memories. I need to move on. My girlfriend sent me here. She was scared I would relapse. I got all depressed when Matthew made the cover of *Q* last month and I started drinking again. She thought I would go back on the cocaine. It's funny how things turn out. Matthew was the junkie when we were in Solarstar, but now he's a fucking celebrity and I'm a has-been, struggling to stay clean. What's your story, man?"

"Alcohol is my drug of choice but my love/hate affair with rock 'n' roll is the real culprit. I can't move forward. I'm thirty-two going on eighteen. I used to be a writer, now I'm nothing."

"Thirty-two, eh? That means you're a pre-seventies man."

"What the hell is a pre-seventies man?"

"It's this theory I have. Dudes who were born in the sixties have a different outlook on life. We grew up on Evel Knievel, Muhammed Ali, and our dads' *Playboy* collections. Punk rock was a religion for guys like us. It wasn't some bullshit Summer of Love phase. I'm not good at anything except writing songs and I'm cool with that now. It sucks that Matthew is dating supermodels and selling out arenas, but his new music sucks. Time won't be kind to him."

"It won't. The Solarstar album is a stone classic."

"I've got to let it go, though. When I get better I want to tour and play the old songs again. There's no way the original band would get together – certainly not Matthew – but I need to get Solarstar out of my system. Sorry for rambling. There's nothing to do here except talk to counselors and shoot the breeze with the inmates."

"And as The Chameleons song goes, smoke funny cigarettes and talk for hours of places that we've seen."

"Fuck, *Intrigue in Tangiers* is one of my favorite songs. You're okay with me, man. The Chameleons influenced us, especially Matthew. He stole the riff from *In Shreds* for *Wrecked*. You know that one, right? The flip side to *Uppers and Downers*."

"Of course. Great song, should have made the album. I love The Chameleons, too. I always wondered what Mark Burgess meant by the funny cigarettes lyric."

"I asked him about that once. He said he was talking about those rollup cigarettes that older English gents favor. I used to roll them with a 50/50 mixture of tobacco and weed when I was on tour. It took the edge off without making me want to fall off the deep end. It worked. I didn't become a full-blown addict until I stopped touring. Rock 'n' roll is supposed to be this gateway to hellish places, but it's the only thing that keeps me sane. That, and traveling to cool places. Speaking of Tangier, have you ever been to Morocco?"

"No."

"It's my favorite place on earth, especially Marrakech. Casablanca is overrated, but you'd love Marrakech. The architecture is bad ass. There are these weird little alleys that lead to nowhere. It's like Venice in the desert. It makes me feel like I'm on another planet. I'd love to retire there; live in a trippy riad, sip mint tea in the courtyard, and listen to music all day."

*

I exit the subway station at Central Square and begin the short walk to the Middle East. When I arrive at the club, Mark's smoking outside. He looks good. He's less pale and thin than he was in rehab, still rocking the perfect haircut. He hugs me. I don't want to let go.

When we do, Mark says, "Holy shit, Drew. I wasn't expecting you until later."

He offers me a hit.

"There's a little weed in there if you're okay with that."

"Works for me."

I take a long drag and say, "To funny cigarettes."

"To funny cigarettes."

Dance Away the Heartache

Mark has time to kill before sound-check, so we head across the street for coffee. When we're settled in our booth, he doesn't mince words.

"Are you good, man?"

I know exactly what he means.

"Yeah, I had one relapse where I started drinking again for a few months but, outside of that, I'm good, other than the occasional toke of weak weed."

"Weed won't kill you. To be honest, it'll probably help more than whatever meds you're on."

"So, holy shit, I still can't believe you reformed Solarstar."

"It's a trip but, as you know, it's not the original band."

"I figured as much."

"We're tight, though. I'm backed by three young cats from L.A. They all play in good bands when they're not jamming with me. They're all ex-Brian Jonestown Massacre members, so nothing fazes them. They've seen it all. They may be young but they're not green."

"I can imagine. I've seen BJM a few times here in Boston. Memorable gigs to say the least."

"So, what have you been up to, Drew? Are you still working for the man?"

"I was until this morning. I just got fired."

I give Mark a quick recap.

"Damn. At least you went down in flames."

"It wasn't exactly a retox gig. The stress was eating me alive. I should have taken your advice."

"Speaking of retox, this is last minute, but what are you doing for the rest of the year?"

"Hell if I know."

"We need someone to sell our merch. Our bass player's girlfriend, who's an actress, was going to do it, but she just landed a minor role on *Dawson's Creek*."

"When do I start?"

"As soon as you can. Ian worked the table last night in New York and he's already had enough. And that was our first gig. He's not big on manual labor."

"Ian as in Ian Gregg?"

"Indeed. The man, the legend."

"Wow. He put out some great records."

"Cherry Smash is still going, just re-issues and garage rock compilations these days. He lives in Los Angeles now, too. He moved there just before I did. It was a good place for us to hide after Solarstar. Anyway, I'll run it by Ian. You'll meet him at sound-check. I'm sure he'll be relieved to hand over merch duties to you. Speaking of, we should probably head back to the club."

When we return to the Middle East, the band is tuning up and engaging in back and forth banter with the stoically patient sound guy, who keeps adjusting levels until everything is satisfactory. Mark joins the group on stage, grabs his guitar, and they kick into the debut single *Uppers and Downers*, an intense rave up which, when released in 1986, made single of the week in the *NME* and *Melody Maker*.

I position myself in the middle of the room. They look and sound great. Being surrounded by handsome wire-thin shaggy-haired guys in their mid-twenties makes Mark appear closer in age, even though he has a good decade on them. He's a modern day Lestat, feeding off his band's youthful energy.

When the sound-check finishes, Mark introduces me to Ian. He's tall and thin with an obviously dyed jet-black Ron Wood haircut, dressed to the nines in a crushed velvet blazer, paisley shirt, and freshly polished Beatle boots.

"Hey Ian, this is Drew, the guy I was telling you about. He's going to sell our merch if you're cool with that."

"Best news I've heard all day," says Ian in a posh London accent. "How soon can you start?"

"Can you give me a few days? I have a few loose ends to tie up."

"We're in Philadelphia tomorrow and then Cleveland a few days after that. Can you make that? Big homecoming gig for our Mark."

"Shit, that's right," I say. "I forgot you grew up there."

"Don't remind me," laughs Mark.

"I can swing it."

"Cool," says Ian. "We'll discuss logistics after the gig."

When the club doors open to concert goers, the band relocates backstage to chill. The drummer Tommy and bass player Skip are knocking back Rolling Rocks, while Mark and Vic, who is taking on Matthew's old role as lead guitarist, pass around a rollup. I take a few more hits. When the support act finishes, I peak outside. The room is packed, a pleasant surprise. I wasn't sure what to expect since Solarstar were never big in America, having only briefly toured here in '88 before crashing and burning Sex Pistols-style in New Orleans.

As I make my way backstage to tell the guys the good news, I notice Emily out of the corner of my eye. She's with a guy I don't know, and I'm reminded of an old Roxy Music song. I'm in no mood to get to the chorus and dance away the heartache, so I avoid eye contact.

Seeing Emily with someone else stings. I'm desperate for a drink. A shot of Jameson would hit the spot. I pull myself together and bum a hit from Mark's rollup.

"Are you okay, man?" he asks.

"Nothing I can't shake. I just saw Emily with someone else. We've been done for ages, but it's hard to see it right in front of me."

"I know the feeling, man."

"Didn't mean to bum you out, Mark. Have a great gig."

"Right on. Rock 'n' roll."

The crowd is a mix of people my age (and older), who discovered the band the first time around, and a smattering of young Britpop kids who buy Matthew St. James's maudlin solo albums in droves, no doubt curious to experience his old partner-in-crime.

Solarstar are barely visible in the smoke machine-generated fog, and immediately dive into *Uppers and Downers*. Vic tears into the opening chords as Mark leans into the mic. He looks cool as fuck in vintage Ray-Bans, skintight leather trousers, and a striped T-shirt. Shards of feedback fill the room and a few kids jump back. You're a long way from Camden, I laugh to myself.

Solarstar play for an hour; the entire album, plus several B-sides. The crowd screams for more and, after the obligatory five-minute wait, the group makes a triumphant return to the stage. Mark takes a few drags from a cigarette and admits that they've already played every song in the Solarstar repertoire.

"Hope you're cool with a couple of covers. Last night in New York we did songs by Suicide and Television, but this isn't the Big Apple, so we've got something different planned for you."

They kick into the Modern Lovers' *She Cracked*, followed by a scorching take of Mission of Burma's *That's When I Reach for My Revolver*. The crowd screams as Solarstar exits the stage, feedback from the amps glaring at near My Bloody Valentine levels.

I walk over to the merch booth to help Ian, who's been selling an impressive number of T-shirts, newly re-issued CDs (with bonus B-side tracks) and, even, a few copies of a limited-edition vinyl pressing.

"That's cool you put it out on wax. Most labels don't bother anymore."

"Because I'm a stubborn git," admits Ian. "I still put out every Cherry Smash release on vinyl. Granted, most of our releases are sixties garage rock compilations and the people in that scene hate CDs. I wasn't sure what to expect with Solarstar, but we sold a handful last night and a few more tonight."

"So, who's running the label while you're here?"

"A lad named Danny Scorpio. He's about your age; a real cool cat. Danny's a walking L.A. rock 'n' roll encyclopedia, everything from Buffalo Springfield and The Byrds through The Gun Club and Jane's Addiction, plus all the new groups who keep popping up. He publishes a fanzine called *Left Coast Underground*. You'd love it. When the tour ends, I'll show you around the office. It's a nice little spot on Melrose."

"That would be awesome."

"Right on. The last date of the tour is at the Troubadour, the weekend before Thanksgiving. I've always loved that venue. I played in a few bands in the sixties, but we never made it to America. I always wanted to visit Los Angeles and meet Love and The Byrds and now I live there, but damn it, I never did play the bloody Troubadour."

"What's the scene like in L.A. these days?"

"It's pretty happening. Danny's more tuned in than I am but there are some great groups knocking about. He keeps bugging me to sign someone, but I've been gun shy to take on a new act since Solarstar split up. I make a decent living playing the reissue game. There's far less drama, too. The old groups are happy to see their records back in print and no longer have ridiculous sales expectations. Old age has a mellowing effect on most artists."

Ian sighs before continuing.

"That said, the rush of watching a young, ambitious band rise to stardom can't be beat. I miss those days, but to answer your question, Brian Jonestown Massacre are probably the best-known underground band in L.A. Outside of that, there's this group called Black Rebel Motorcycle Club. They're a trio who dress in black head to toe, the perfect marriage of The Stooges and The Jesus and Mary Chain. Danny is sold on them and was bugging me to sign them for months. It looks like they've landed a big deal with Virgin, though. I can't compete with that kind of money. The Warlocks are another great act. They're loud and psychedelic. They even have two drummers! Very theatrical."

"Far out. Are they signed?"

"Greg Shaw just inked them to Bomp. He's putting out an EP next year. Maybe it's time for me to add some new groups to the roster, after all. I'll talk to Danny when I get back. Seeing Mark perform again, even with a new lineup, has gotten me nostalgic about the old days."

"I can imagine. I can't wait to check out L.A. I've never been there."

"It's not for everyone. You'll either love it or hate it. It's expensive and can be soul destroying at times, but there's a lot of magic in the air and it's beautiful. It's full of beaches and canyons, nothing like that in England. So, are you doing any writing these days? Mark told me that you used to write for *Spin*."

"No, but I've been feeling the urge to do so again. Joining you guys on tour is the best thing that's happened to me in ages. I'd love to document it somehow, maybe do a few interviews with you and

Mark to get your side of the Solarstar story. I'm tired of reading about Matthew fucking St. James."

"You and me both," laughs Ian, "but that would be great. I love to talk about the old days. Not just my youth when I was hanging out in London with the Stones and Pretty Things. The eighties had their moments, too. I was in my forties then but, unlike a lot of my contemporaries, I was still going to gigs and discovering new bands."

"I lived in England in '85 and '86. We possibly crossed paths a few times."

"Where were you staying?"

"I was at the University of Essex in Colchester but got to London as much as I could. I moved to Ireland in the summer of '86 with the girl who would become my ex-wife. We saw Solarstar in Dublin."

"Mark told me about that."

"Seems so long ago," I say, saddened by the memory.

Throughout our animated conversation, Ian and I manage the booth like a couple of seasoned carnies. I'm grabbing merch for the fans, while Ian handles the cash flow. As the crowd inside the club dwindles, Emily and her new man make their way to the table. She buys a T-shirt and CD. New guy, who is introduced as Benjamin – only fops call themselves Benjamin – buys nothing and looks bored. He's too clean cut and conservative for Emily; he's wearing boat shoes for fuck's sake. I blame myself. I'm certain I've put her off rock 'n' roll guys for life.

"I see you already found a new job?" jokes Emily.

"Indeed, I have. I'm going to be managing the merch booth for the rest of the tour."

Emily looks surprised and shaken.

"What about your job at the bank?"

"I just got fired."

"Oh shit. I'm so sorry. Are you okay?"

I'm more than okay; I'm high as a kite.

"Yeah," I say. "Getting out of Boston will be good for me."

"This is so sudden. How long will you be gone?"

"The tour ends just after Thanksgiving."

"Take care of yourself then and I'll see you when you get back."

Emily gives me a long hug and a quick kiss on the lips. Benjamin squirms. I cry a little inside, knowing that it's all over. I have no plans to return.

The Terminator

The next day I phone my landlord, telling him that I've been offered a job I can't refuse in Los Angeles. He's surprisingly cool but, then again, this is Boston. He'll be able to rent my place out in less than twenty minutes. I sit on the floor and rifle through the record collection. Time to downsize. All the vinyl I can't live without – Bunnymen, Mary Chain, Sisters of Mercy, Psych Furs – goes into a box, which my brother says I can store at his place. Most of my CDs are freebies that I've hung on to since my writing days, too lazy to sell off to used record stores. Now's the time. I box up a good five hundred and phone the Terminator.

The Terminator is a fanatical record collector named Stephen. He's short, stocky, and has a nervous disposition. A friend christened him the Terminator because of his OCD habits. Whenever the Terminator discovers a new act, he manages to track down the group's entire back catalogue – albums, EPs, compilation cuts, the full Monty – with the precision of a hired assassin. His apartment is like a museum with custom built shelves and framed limited-edition gig posters. His other claim to fame is an impeccably clean kitchen. I once asked how he kept it so pristine. His response was that he never cooked, that he sustained himself on Healthy Choice microwave dinners.

The Terminator arrives.

"Dude, your place looks like a ghost town!"

"Emily took all the stuff when she moved out. Story of my life when it comes to women."

I direct him to my sell pile. He plows through the collection, cross referencing CDs he's interested in with a wish list stored on his PalmPilot.

"I've been guilty of buying stuff I already own on more than one occasion," he admits.

The Terminator's taking his sweet ass time and I'm getting antsy, knowing I have a few errands to run.

"So, how about a grand for the whole lot?" I ask. "You can easily sell what you already own and make a nice profit."

"Eight hundred and it's a deal."

"Works for me."

We load the CDs into the Terminator's Corolla and drive to the bank. Twenty minutes later I'm flush in cash. Between that and my severance pay, I'll be okay for the rest of the year.

Stiv Bators Died for Your Sins

My brother drives me to Logan Airport. He's only three years older than me, but it feels like we're from different planets, brothers from different mothers. Paul is a newly-tenured political science professor at the best university in America, a rising star in his world. He's the same age as Mark, but his career is on an upward spiral, while Mark's glory days are long gone, a once shining (solar)star in descent. I wonder if my best years are behind me, too. I'm thirty-four with nothing to my name other than bylines in music magazines and several unsuccessful tours of duty at dead-end office jobs.

Paul and I don't say much on the drive, just idle chit chat, until he asks if I've talked to Mom and Dad. I say I have, that they seem disappointed.

"I can't say I blame them. I thought you were okay. Well, other than Emily. I know that hurts. I wish you'd talk to me. I know you've had a rough time, but so have I. My divorce sucked, but I'm dating again. I want to find the right girl and start a family. Don't you?"

"I don't know. I just feel like running away."

"You've been doing that your whole life, Drew. Stop being so selfish. Mom and Dad keep blaming themselves. You've hurt them so much."

"Because I'm an alcoholic ex-writer instead of a straight arrow professor?"

"Get over it, Drew. They were tough on me, too, but I'm glad I listened to them."

"So you didn't have to turn out like me?"

Paul looks so grown up as he lays into me, like a father scolding his young boy. He's wearing a Harris tweed jacket and a freshly-pressed button down, an Ivy League rock star. In contrast, I'm in jeans, black T-shirt, and a black motorcycle jacket, forever twenty-one, but I feel free. Yesterday, I donated two garbage bags worth of office clothes to Goodwill and it felt like a noose had been loosened.

I take Paul's 'advice' with a grain of salt, but his words eat at me on the flight. I didn't set out to destroy myself when I fell in love with rock 'n' roll. I pop another Valium and gaze out at the clear blue sky from my window seat. Every minute further from Boston feels like a minor victory.

I land at Cleveland Hopkins in the early afternoon and take a cab to the offices of *Alternative Press* magazine, located in a sketchy section on the city's west side. Solarstar are there when I arrive, getting their photos taken for an upcoming feature. I'm introduced to the managing editor Rob Cherry, who has assigned me stories in the past, but this is the first time we've met in the flesh.

"Nice to meet you, Drew. First time in Cleveland?"

"Yes. I've driven through here but never stopped."

"No reason to," wisecracks someone in the background.

I'm offered a cup of coffee and scarf down a semi-stale donut.

"So," says Rob, "I was talking to Ian and Mark and they mentioned that you wanted to write something about Solarstar, like Mark's side of the story."

Mark removes his shades and says, "Hope I'm not putting you on the spot, man, but I asked Rob if you could interview me."

"It's cool with me if you're up for it," says Rob.

"Uh, sure," I say, as I gather my thoughts. "So, when's my deadline?"

"Like, yesterday," laughs Rob. "We can record it in my office now and one of our interns will transcribe it. We'll publish it old school Q&A style like *Interview* magazine, since you're going to be on the road."

"Sure," I say as my brain races for questions to ask Mark. I follow them to a conference room down the hall. When we're seated around the table, Rob turns on his recorder, checks the sound levels, and we begin.

*

DREW: Mark, I know you're from Cleveland, but when's the last time you were here?

MARK: Uh, that would have been '88 when Solarstar played this little club called the Phantasy. It's this weird joint with a giant pirate ship inside. The support band that night was some small-time local band called Nine Inch Nails. Wonder what happened to those guys?

DREW: Ha! So, what was your childhood like? How did you get into music?

MARK: I'm from Bay Village, a ritzy west side suburb. I was your typical seventies kid. I played little league baseball and was an honor student through junior high school, until my dad died. I was fourteen when that happened, the summer of '76. My dad fell asleep behind the wheel on his way home from work and crashed into a tree. He was a partner at a law firm and worked all the fucking time. The job literally killed him. My mom became a born-again Christian and I escaped into music. I got way into Alice Cooper and

David Bowie and started hanging out with the stoners. My mom was too drugged up on Jesus and diet pills to give a shit.

DREW: Is that when you started playing?

MARK: More or less. I bought an acoustic at a garage sale after my dad died. I had a book that taught me the basic chords and I'd play along to the radio. Within a few months I could play anything. I didn't think about being in a band back then. When I was a sophomore I met a girl named Kristi, who moved here from New York City. Her dad was a scientist at the NASA plant out by the airport. She was the first punk I met. She had spiky, bleached blonde hair and wore short skirts and fishnets. We met in detention the first week of school. She was there for a dress code violation. I was there for skipping class. I used to cut class a lot. My friends and I would get high in the parking lot and drive to My Generation, which was the best record store on our side of town.

DREW: They should have given you extra credit for that!

MARK: I wish. Anyway, Kristi and I hit it off. She couldn't believe that I didn't know who The Dead Boys were since they formed in Cleveland. She had seen them and countless other groups like Blondie, Television, Patti Smith, and The Ramones at CBGB. She was fifteen going on twenty-five, a real wild child. We went to her house after detention and she played me *Young Loud and Snotty*. I lost my virginity to her. Not that day, but a few weeks later. After that, she cut my hair, like I was the newest butterfly in her collection. I still think about her a lot. She had an electric guitar and an amp and after the haircut, I asked if I could play. I nailed down *Sonic Reducer* and I think that's how I won her over. We'd sneak into clubs, cut class to get high with the stoners, all the delinquent high school shit. Her parents hated me. The next year, they sent her to an all-girls school out east. When she left, Kristi gave me the guitar and amp. She said, "This guitar is going to save your life or kill you. Use it wisely." Deep words from such a young girl but, then again, she dabbled in poetry.

DREW: Wow. Did you see her again?

MARK: Yeah. We exchanged letters and we'd hang out when she came home for the holidays. The last time I heard from her was just before I graduated high school in 1980. She wrote to say that she was coming back to Ohio, that she was going to college at Oberlin. I never wrote back. Biggest regret of my life. I moved to New York City the day after graduation. I didn't want to go to college and if I stayed in Cleveland I would have held her back. She had this tough punk girl exterior, but she was a straight-A student. I figured she'd meet some well-adjusted dude at Oberlin and forget about me. I'm sure she has.

DREW: That's so sad.

MARK: I know. I fucked up bad. I was a dumbass. I owe her a lot. God knows where I'd be if I hadn't met my punk poet in detention?

DREW: Were you in any other bands before Solarstar?

MARK: A few, but none of them did much. I know Cleveland and Akron have this punk rock reputation because of groups like The Dead Boys, Devo, and Pere Ubu, but us punks were a lonely breed. The good bands would move out of town. Cleveland isn't kind to creative people. At least it wasn't back then.

DREW: How did you end up working for The Lords of the New Church?

MARK: When I got to New York, I moved into a dive in the Bowery. I got a job washing dishes and started seeing as many gigs as I could. It wasn't what I expected. The CBGB scene was long gone and all these violent hardcore groups were playing the circuit. I felt like I was back in Cleveland again; a musician with a plan but no one to share it with. In '81, I met a dude who was friends with Stiv Bators. He told me that Stiv had a new group called The Lords of the New Church and that they needed a roadie. I got the gig, and, at times, I felt like I was their fucking nanny. I'd lug gear, tune guitars, score drugs, and invite women backstage. I even did their fucking laundry.

DREW: When did you meet Matthew St. James?

MARK: I met Matthew in London in '84 when the Lords were touring *Method to Our Madness*. Life on the road was a drag. I wanted to be in a cool band, like Stiv. I recorded a three-song demo at a crappy studio in New York, hoping I might connect with kindred spirits in England. Matthew was in the group who supported the Lords that night. They were called The Gems. The singer was pretentious as fuck, but Matthew was the shit.

DREW: So, did you talk to him that night?

MARK: Yeah. We hung out at the after party. Our tastes were identical. We loved the punk icons like The Stooges, Damned, and Dead Boys, but we also liked artsier shit like The Velvet Underground, Only Ones, and The Psychedelic Furs – Matthew worshipped John Ashton's guitar sound on those early Furs records. He told me that he was going to leave The Gems and I said that he would love my demo. I gave him a cassette that night. I'd always carry a few on me, like they were my business cards. He loved the songs and bought me a one-way ticket to London in the summer of '85. His family was loaded. They owned a huge estate near Brighton and Matthew had an entire wing to himself. He had a home studio set up and we banged out ten songs. After that, we poached Bobby and Chris, the rhythm section from The Gems, and formed the group.

DREW: How did you chance on the name Solarstar?

MARK: At the time Matthew was obsessed with Brian Jones and other blonde icons like Monroe, Warhol, and Iggy Pop. When we finished recording the demos Matthew and I moved into a flat in Camden with Bobby and Chris. We were like the punk Monkees; dirty dishes everywhere, girls coming in and out at all hours. Matthew and I got really stoned one night and he was like, 'It's time to christen the group.' We rifled through his collection, searching for inspiration. Out of the corner of my eye, I noticed the Psychic TV *Godstar* single. I picked it up and gazed at the Brian Jones collage on the sleeve. We both whispered, "Godstar." We were like, that's perfect but too obvious. We loved the star part, so we tossed around variations of spacey names until landing on Solarstar.

DREW: How long did it take to get signed?

MARK: A few months. The Gems connection got us gigs with the Mary Chain, Loop, My Bloody Valentine, and Spacemen 3. The press lumped us in with that scene. Mark and I favored leather trousers, worn with striped T-shirts or black turtlenecks. We lived in our black leather jackets. It was our tribute to The Velvet Underground and the New York scene. Alan McGee liked us a lot, but he had just signed The House of Love to Creation and didn't have the funds. Ian Gregg loved us and offered us a deal.

DREW: What were your first impressions of Ian? Was he a total dandy then, too?

MARK: Even more so, man. His office was a trip, like we'd stepped into the sixties. He had all this vintage furniture and lava lamps. He dimmed down the lights and we signed away our lives under a ganja haze. We barely read the contract but, thankfully, Ian followed Tony Wilson's model at Factory where profits were split evenly. The album was recorded in a fortnight on a steady diet of coffee, speed, weed, and pot noodles.

DREW: *Uppers and Downers* was your first single. I remember it causing quite a stir.

MARK: We got a lot of press. It was the single of the week in *NME* and *Melody Maker*. It's not my favorite song on the record – in retrospect, too '77 Dead Boys/Damned-influenced – but it was the punchiest song on the album. The launch party was great. Ian booked us at the Marquee. It was his favorite venue in the sixties. There were a lot of faces in the crowd, including Johnny Marr. Afterwards, we went to this party at a swank hotel suite. Matthew and Johnny went into a corner and talked vintage guitars all night, while I got bombed. Stiv popped in and told me I was great. I was so proud. I was no longer this punk rock loser from Cleveland.

DREW: What are some of your fondest memories from the early days?

MARK: The first tour was a blast. We had this crap white van with a broken heater. Our driver was an ex-con from Ulster named Stewart, a real hard man. He'd tell us stories about people he shanked in prison, we never knew what to believe. I still laugh when I think about him. Our first gig was in Brighton and these girls from the university took us around town that afternoon. Matthew and I hammed it up and got our photo taken with a bell boy in front of the Grand Hotel, our homage to *Quadrophenia*. I still have it. At times, touring can be a drag; you know, that endless cycle of motorways, Little Chef for tea, sound checks in dingy venues, but the gigs were great. Something was wrong with Matthew though. It took me a while to notice that he was using again. I knew that he was shooting up when he was in The Gems, but he was clean when we recorded the album. I was so pissed off, man. Simon Reynolds from *Melody Maker* had just written that *Solarstar* was the best debut since *Psychocandy* and here I was, wondering if we were through.

DREW: I remember nothing but stories about canceled gigs after the album came out.

MARK: The European tour sucked. Ian hired a roadie to be Matthew's minder and keep him clean. When we arrived in Amsterdam, Matthew disappeared and didn't turn up until right before we were due on. The three of us were shitting ourselves, trying to figure out how to play as a three piece. I'm a good guitarist but I'm no Johnny Marr. Matthew was in that class, even when he was off his tits. We sucked that night. For the first time ever, we were booed. When we got backstage, Chris and Bobby started doing lines off a mirror and I completely lost it. I punched the mirror so hard that it shattered. There was blood gushing all over the place. I had to go to ER to get stitched up.

DREW: Wow. I never heard that story.

MARK: We kept it under wraps. Well, until now. When we returned to London, Matthew checked into rehab.

DREW: I remember that. You had to go on *Top of the Pops* without him.

MARK: Which sucked. Matthew grew up on that show. I was an American kid, so it wasn't a big deal for me, but *Top of the Pops* is the shit if you're English. We played our latest single *Bullet*, which peaked at number nine in the UK charts. It's the best thing I've ever written. When I visited Matthew in rehab, he told me that he watched us on *Top of the Pops* and wept for hours. I was so bummed out.

DREW: *Bullet* is my favorite Solarstar song. It reminds me of *Shivers*.

MARK: Thanks, man. That's a huge compliment. Rowland S. Howard wrote *Shivers* when he was a kid and *Bullet* was one of the first songs I ever wrote. It was on that original three-song demo I gave to Matthew. It's about Kristi. As trite as the chorus is – "One day I'll die for you" – it sounded sincere coming from an angst-ridden seventeen-year-old. Matthew fucked it all up. I wish we could have toured America when the coals were hot – some of the big stations like KROQ were playing *Bullet* on heavy rotation – but we had to wait until he got better.

DREW: So, what were you doing during this break?

MARK: I was trying to write new songs, but I couldn't do shit. I felt like half a person without Matthew. I visited him in rehab most days and I'd cheer him up with lies, telling him that I had written new songs that needed his touch.

DREW: Let me know if any of this needs to be off the record.

MARK: No, it's all good, man.

DREW: Speaking of, did you ever resolve that spat with Jane's Addiction? I remember you guys felt like they ripped off *Strung Out Sister*.

MARK: Ah, right. I forgot about that. Jane's released their debut about a month after our record came out. Matthew thought *Jane Says* ripped off our second single *Strung Out Sister* and said some nasty things about Perry in the press. When Matthew was in rehab, someone in Jane's – can't remember who – said some mean shit about us. When I moved to L.A. I met Perry. By then *Ritual* was out and they were massive. I told Perry that my song was about a junkie girlfriend I had in New York, someone I'd crash with when I wasn't touring with the Lords. Perry told me his story about Jane. We were just a couple of Velvet Underground-fixated dudes with junkie muses. Two chords and the truth!

DREW: Which leads us to the American tour.

MARK: Right. It started great. Matthew was healthy again. He even took up running. Our first gig was in New York and it was awesome – it reminded me of that night at the Marquee – but, soon after, Matthew fell off the wagon and started drinking. We let it slide, justifying that at least it wasn't smack. We were getting worse as the tour dragged on. Nine Inch Nails blew us off the stage in Cleveland. Our last gig ever was in New Orleans at a dive in the French Quarter. It was like that horrible night in Amsterdam. Matthew could barely stand, so we seated him on a stool – he fell and shit his pants. The crowd booed us off stage. When we got backstage, Matthew ran into the night, like a crazed nocturnal creature. We figured he'd score and eventually turn up, but he never did. I phoned Ian, who was in L.A., and he canceled the remaining dates and hired a detective to look for Matthew. We hung out in New Orleans for a few days waiting for scoops. The detective had nothing, so we gunned it to L.A. The police eventually found Matthew wandering around in the hot sun in New Orleans. Apparently, he had been hospitalized but ripped out his IVs and escaped!

DREW: So, that was the end?

MARK: Yeah. Matthew got the help he needed and has remained clean to this day. I moved back to London and got a solo deal with Warner Brothers. It took forever to record my album, which, thankfully, never saw the light of day. The label hated the record so much that they dropped me without releasing it.

DREW: When did you move to L.A.?

MARK: In '91. I had no reason to stay in England. I needed to get as far away from London as I could. I reconnected with Ian, who had just moved there. He tried to keep me straight, but I was a fucking mess. I was getting decent royalty checks, especially for *Bullet*, which had been used in a few movies, but I'd blow most of the money on coke. In '93 I played a gig at the Viper Room. I was so wasted that I couldn't remember the words to any of my songs, so I started doing Dead Boys covers. It felt like an out of body experience, like I had become my sixteen-year-old self, playing along to Kristi's record collection. A guy in the crowd started heckling me. He kept yelling, 'Stiv Bators died for your sins!' I jumped off the stage and smashed an empty beer bottle on his head. I spent the night in jail. The next day I checked into rehab.

DREW: Any plans to record a second Solarstar album?

MARK: No. This tour has been great, and I love the new guys, but this is it for Solarstar. When the tour ends I'm going to finish my solo album. I don't know what else to do. It's not like I can go work at Taco Bell.

Ain't It Fun

We return to the main office, where Ian and the band are having beers with the *AP* staff. Someone asks about Elliott Smith, who currently resides in L.A., and Tommy fills them in.

"Elliott's a mess, as usual, but I hear that the follow up to *XO* is finally done. He hangs out at this dive in Atwater Village called the Roost. I like going there because they pour super strong drinks. It's dimly lit with these cool red leather booths, very old school. Elliott likes to keep to himself, but there's this group of girls who are obsessed with him and hang out there all the time. They won't leave him alone when he's around."

I grow nostalgic for a similar joint I used to frequent in Cambridge and start to jones for a drink. I ask Skip for a cigarette – just a regular Marlboro Red – and head outside. I pop a Valium and swallow it down with as much saliva as I can muster. Mark joins me.

"Doing okay there, man?"

"Not sure. I just had a weird panic attack and needed air. I get that way when I'm around too much alcohol these days, like a claustrophobia thing."

"News flash, Drew. Musicians like drugs."

"I'll survive."

"Don't bottle it inside. We need to look out for each other. You should crash with me when the tour ends. There's a spare bedroom in my house."

"That would be great, but I thought you were living with your girlfriend, the one you told me about in rehab. Sorry, I forgot her name."

"Ah, Jessica. We split up months ago. The tour was a deal breaker. She's convinced that I'm going to relapse."

"That sucks."

"It did for a while, but she wasn't the right one. She's super successful. She runs an ad agency. We're too different."

"So, what brought you together in the first place?"

"AA. I know. I dissed it all the time in rehab, but a few years ago I hit a low point and started going to meetings. That's how we met. She's sold on the program, so it was a sore point for her when I'd skip meetings. When I started drinking again – right before I met you – she was so pissed. She said she'd break up with me if I didn't start going to AA again, but I don't need God in my life. I need rock 'n' roll. Anyway, the guest room is yours if you want it."

"I'd love it. Where do you live?"

"In Hollywood. You'll get a kick out of this, since you're from Michigan. I live on a street called Detroit. It's a ten-minute walk to Ian's office. I go there most mornings to have coffee with Ian."

"Sounds nice."

"It is. Routine is important. You need to establish one when the tour ends. It's a lifesaver. I have a small recording studio in my house. I work on songs most days and I've been recording demos for some new bands I like. There's a group I especially dig called Smallstone. They're great looking guys, who dress like they've time-traveled from mid-sixties London. You know, velvet blazers, silk scarves. You'd love them."

"Looking forward to the gig tonight?"

"Yeah, but I'm nervous as shit. You know, playing the old home town and all that."

"Any friends coming out?"

"I doubt it. I burned some bridges when I moved to New York and I don't have family here anymore."

"What about your mom?"

"She died a few years ago."

"Shit. I'm sorry."

"Thanks, man. She moved to Phoenix to live with my aunt. She disowned me after I moved to New York. My dad left money in his will for me to go to college, but I had no interest. My mom was so pissed off. She was off her rocker on Jesus and thought Satan was holding me hostage. She died from lung cancer. I guess that's why I'm sensitive about cigarettes. I know I'm a hypocrite since I smoke on stage, but that's because I get nervous when I'm out of my element. I like to stay in my little neighborhood in Hollywood, where I can walk everywhere. So, stub out that fucking cigarette. Only funny cigarettes allowed on my watch."

"Yes, sir!"

"Damn straight. Doctor's orders."

"Okay, Dr. Rock."

"Ha! I like it, but don't tell the other guys. Everyone in the band has picked up a fucking nickname, except me. I'd like to keep it that way."

"So, what are the other nicknames?"

"Skip is the Urinator because he has a bladder the size of a fucking field mouse. It's reached the point where Ian makes him piss into empty Gatorade bottles in the back of the van. I swear, Skip was making us stop every hour on the drive from New York to Boston. Vic is the Tape Master because he has such impeccable taste in music. He has a fantastic record collection and has made some incredible mixes for this tour. Tommy is Granola because he's a vegan and a health nut, other than the fact that he drinks a shit ton of beer."

"Ha, I love it. What about Ian?"

"We call him the Count, but don't dare say it to his face."

"As in Count Dracula?"

"Exactly. Ian is a notorious womanizer. He's been divorced three times. He has a specific type; young mod girls in their twenties, though he'll settle on anyone under thirty who gives him a valid phone number. Never mind that he's probably older than most of their dads. After our New York gig, the venue we played at turned into a goth club. Ian was making the rounds with a glass of brandy in his hand. The DJ put on *Bela Lugosi's Dead*. We were all sitting at a table shooting the shit while Ian was scoping the room. When Peter Murphy sang that bit about the Count, Skip blurted out, 'Ian's the fucking Count, look at him!' Again, you're sworn to secrecy. Ian would kill us if he found out."

Mark lights up a funny cigarette and takes a long drag before offering me a hit. I decline. My nerves are steady again. The Count joins us, saying that it's time to head to the club for the soundcheck.

The concert is at an east side dive called the Grog Shop, which opened after Mark left town. Rob Cherry, who rides in the van with us, tells us that it's great, that he's seen BJM, Oasis, and Dinosaur, Jr. there. He warns us that the bathroom is disgusting, that it might be better to piss in the alley.

"Can't be worse than CBGB," says Mark.

The club lives up to expectation, gross bathroom and all. I watch the soundcheck, marveling at how tight the band is. Vic is a fantastic guitarist, perfectly nailing Matthew's parts but, unlike Matthew, he won't be drugged up tonight.

After soundcheck, Mark goes backstage to take a nap on a weathered couch. Vic asks if I want to join him for a slice of pizza. He's played at the Grog Shop before and knows a nice little joint up the street called Tommy's.

When we're seated, Vic asks what I thought of the show the other night.

"I thought you were great," I say. "Better than the original lineup I saw in Dublin in '87. Matthew was a mess. You guys sound like the records."

"I appreciate you saying that. Solarstar were my favorite band in high school. I was seventeen when their album came out. I played it non-stop along with Spacemen 3 and anything I could get my hands on from New Zealand."

"Like The Chills and Straitjacket Fits?"

"Man, you're speaking my language. I could go on forever about Flying Nun Records. I'd love to visit New Zealand and pay my respects."

Vic has an intense look on his face, as if he were a scholar defending his thesis in front of an academic committee.

"So, how well do you know Mark?" Vic asks.

"Pretty well, I guess. We were in rehab together two years ago. We lost touch, but after hanging out with him in Boston and doing the interview today, I feel like I've known him forever."

"Was it a good interview?"

"Yeah. He told some amazing stories. How do you know him? I didn't ask how he got the current lineup together."

"I used to be in the Brian Jonestown Massacre when they were based in San Francisco. Mark saw us play in Los Angeles in '94, just after *Hide and Seek* came out. I told him how much I loved Solarstar and we became instant friends. I ended up moving to L.A. two years ago for a girl. We broke up six months ago, but Mark and I reconnected and started jamming in his studio. When Ian decided to reissue the album, and set up a tour, Mark asked if I'd be the lead guitarist. I still can't believe my luck. I recruited Skip and Tommy. They're in a country rock band called Catalina Coast, but I know them from BJM circles. I'm still good friends with

Anton, even though I quit his band. Skip and Tommy played a few gigs with BJM before Catalina Coast took off. Anton has a revolving door membership these days, but he's been writing some great songs. Greg Shaw is releasing a new album next year."

"That's great news. It's been a while since they've put out a record. Is the tambourine player Joel still in the band? I loved his onstage antics when I saw them in Boston."

"No. He's back in San Francisco. I may move back there, too, unless Mark decides to take the Solarstar show abroad."

"That would be nice, but I don't think Mark thinks that far ahead. You know, one day at a time."

"I hear you. Is it tough being sober?"

"Yeah. I cheat with weed but, unlike what Nancy Reagan might tell you, it's not a gateway drug. At least not for me."

"I'm with you on that. I never drink on tour. It fucks with my stomach too much. It's hard enough to eat well on the road and I can't deal with hangovers. I guess I'm getting old. I turn thirty next year."

"Hell, you're just a kid. I turn thirty-five in January."

"What are you going to do when the tour ends?"

"I'm not sure. I'd like to stay in Los Angeles if I can get a job. Mark offered me his guest room."

"Cool. You'll like it. At least for a while. Everyone does."

"That's what I keep hearing."

"It depends on your situation. Los Angeles is great if you're rich but if you're an aspiring musician like me, you've got to hustle. I keep quitting crappy day jobs to tour with different bands, so I'm broke all the time. I imagine it's the same for you as a writer."

"It used to be. I had a straight office job for the last two years, but I just got fired, so I'm back to square one."

The club is packed when Solarstar come on. It's a small venue, so I have a decent view from the merch booth. I'm having fun working the table and talking to visitors, especially the girls. I've been out of the game for too long and it feels nice to flirt again. Maybe it's the weed I smoked with Vic earlier in the evening, but for once I'm not thinking about Emily.

Solarstar kill it, leaving Mark's hometown crowd breathless. I wonder how it will feel for him when the tour winds down. The songs are over a decade old and it might not be healthy for him to continue to rehash the past. The crowd stomps and claps for a few minutes until the group returns on stage.

"Most of you know that I'm from Cleveland," says Mark.

The crowd yells.

"My favorite band of all-time is The Dead Boys."

The crowd screams. They're putty in his hands.

"I lost my virginity to *Young Loud and Snotty*."

More screams.

"We're going to play a few Dead Boys songs with a very special guest. Ladies and gentlemen, Mr. Cheetah Chrome!"

Cheetah's been at the club for most of the evening. He's visiting from Nashville, where he currently resides. I've been watching him make the rounds, patiently stopping to chat with the old punks, no doubt desperate to revisit their glory days. Mark told me that Clevelanders love to talk about the past and wax nostalgic about the once-great city.

"There's a reason why I left this shit-hole town," said Mark. "The people who stay here are fucking cupcakes."

Cheetah plugs in his guitar and the band immediately rip into *Sonic Reducer*. Cheetah takes the lead with Vic on rhythm. The soaring intro, which sounds like a rocket ship taking off at full speed, drives the crowd into a frenzy. People as old as their forties and fifties bounce around the room, like kids at an all-ages show. Mark nails the vocals, especially the chorus, which is the perfect 'Fuck You' to everyone from Cleveland who didn't believe in The Dead Boys or, in this case, Mark. Mark's out of breath when they finish, and he struggles to catch his wind.

"Did you like that?" he gasps.

The crowd yells.

Someone shouts, "Hey, Cheetah is it good to be back in Cleveland?"

"Not really."

The crowd laughs.

"We have one more for you," says Mark. "Cheetah, are you having fun?

"I'm having fun," he deadpans.

"Well, let's have some fun," says Mark as Cheetah strums the slow-burning intro to *Ain't it Fun*, the supreme closer on the second and final Dead Boys record *We Have Come for Your Children*. Mark looks possessed – like he's become another person – when he sings the part about knowing you're going to die young. Perhaps, he's channeling the self-destructive spirit of Stiv Bators, who died when he was just forty. He even mimics Stiv's live antic where he would pretend to hang himself. As the song nears its finale, Mark removes his T-shirt, wipes his face, and tosses it aside. I brace myself for the onslaught of satisfied punters, who raid the merch both like Viking pillagers.

Death Trip

After the gig, we drive to a Holiday Inn in the suburbs, located just off the motorway. The plan is to sleep until noon checkout before gunning it to St. Andrew's Hall in Detroit, just a three-hour drive. Ian's booked two rooms. One for Skip, Tommy, and Vic. The other for us older guys. Ian orders a bottle of wine from room service, while Mark and I pass around a joint. We're too drained to talk much, but it's a nice moment. I feel like my old self, once again consumed by rock 'n' roll.

It's barely sunrise when Mark taps my shoulder. Ian's dead to the world, snoring up a storm.

"Are you awake, Drew?"

I'm disoriented and could use a few more hours of sleep.

"I am now. What's up?"

"There's something I need to do. Want to go for a drive."

"Uh, okay," I say, wondering what Mark could be contemplating at such an ungodly hour.

"Nothing sinister. I promise. We're only a few miles from my old house in Bay Village. I want to see it. I have no reason to visit Cleveland again. I could use the closure."

He seems choked up as he grabs the keys from the nightstand next to Ian's bed. We head north for a few miles until we dead-end on Lake Avenue. Mark parks the van and we walk past several houses before stopping in front of an impressive two-story home, partially obscured by enormous trees. A brand-new metallic silver Lexus SUV is parked in the driveway, spoiling the otherwise serene setting.

"Home sweet home," says Mark. "I loved this place when I was a kid. All the houses on this side of the street have fantastic backyard views of Lake Erie. It's like a fucking ocean, man. Canada is on the other side, but it's too far away to see, even on the clearest day. I miss that. I used to love watching the fireworks every fourth of July and playing catch with my dad. I've been living in huge, dirty cities since I was eighteen. It's easy to forget how beautiful this planet can be."

"Looks nice. This neighborhood reminds me of where I grew up in Ann Arbor, minus the lake."

"What does your old man do?"

"He's a professor. He's in his sixties now, so he'll be retiring soon. That's going to be tough for him. He loves his job."

"Maybe that's the secret," says Mark. "My dad hated his. Like I said before, it killed him. He would get so upset when he had to work overtime and miss my little league games. He was a huge sports guy. He loved the Cleveland Indians. I wasn't a bad ball player. I was the starting shortstop on my little league and junior high teams and my coach thought I had the potential to play in college. My dad was so proud. I quit sports when he died. I was so lonely and depressed. I almost flunked my freshman year of high school because I skipped school so much. Kristi and punk rock saved me. My dad was forty when he died, the same age as Stiv when he passed. I think about that a lot. The two most influential men in my life were a straight-laced lawyer, who loved baseball, and a junkie rock star."

When we get back to the hotel, Mark and I hang out in the lobby and drink endless cups of coffee, waiting for the rest of the crew to rise and shine. The drive to

Detroit is uneventful, until we enter the city. It looks like a post-apocalyptic movie set as I gaze at the demolished buildings, boarded up homes, and homeless men huddled around garbage can fires. The Urinator only needs one piss stop, which Mark and I are thankful for, considering how much coffee we downed at the hotel.

It's an emotional experience for me when we load in at St. Andrew's. This is the venue where I saw my first club concerts as a nineteen-year-old with a freshly-acquired fake ID; all-time favorites, like The Psychedelic Furs, Echo and the Bunnymen, and The Sisters of Mercy. I even interviewed the latter when my best friend at the time sold them drugs and told their manager I wrote for *Spin*. My college newspaper published the piece, which in a way set the course for my dysfunctional adult life.

I hear The Stooges. At first, I think it's the house stereo before realizing that it's a band sound checking. I go into the main room and see four identically dressed guys, who appear to be in their mid-twenties, belting out *No Fun*. They look like a street gang. They're all in jeans, motorcycle boots, and black T-shirts. The singer's hair is bleached blonde, like Iggy Pop.

Ian joins me and says, "That's a damn good cover. Wonder if they have any decent originals."

When the band finishes, the singer walks over to us.

"Sorry, man. Are we running late? Do you guys need to soundcheck?"

"No hurry," says Ian. "Damn fine rendition of *No Fun*. Do you have any good originals?"

"Hell, yeah," says the singer. "Want to hear one? You're Ian Gregg, right?"

"Uh, yes," says Ian. "How did you know?"

"You played guitar in The Lemon Splash. My uncle is a huge garage rock collector. He has your singles. I'm Eddie," he says, reaching out his hand. "Eddie Zane."

"Nice to meet you," says Ian. "I'm flattered that you've heard of The Lemon Splash. This is Drew. He's a writer and Solarstar's publicist."

I wonder where Ian's heading with his white lie. Is he interested in signing the band and using me as bait?

"Far out," says Eddie. "Nice to meet you."

"Likewise," I say. "Are you from Detroit? I grew up in Ann Arbor."

"Right on. We're all from Detroit or the neighboring suburbs. My uncle went to college in Ann Arbor in the sixties. He introduced me to The Stooges and MC5. He saw The Stooges at the Union the day Danny Fields signed them to Elektra."

"So, what are you called?" asks Ian.

"We're Death Trip."

Eddie signals the other guys to come over, like he's a finger-snapping gang leader in *West Side Story* or *Grease* and makes the introductions. The rest of the band are shy. Eddie is the clear ringmaster. The bass player Spence and guitarist Eric look like they could be brothers, both sporting identical shag haircuts and long sideburns, while the drummer, who is introduced as Chinaski, is quite muscular with multiple tattoos, exposed by his ripped, sleeveless T-shirt. He looks like a bouncer or mechanic.

The band play one of their songs and it's amazing. You can tell that they're influenced by the Motor City hard rock sound, but there's something modern to them, too. I can hear traces of The Jesus and Mary Chain circa *Honey's Dead*; Stooges riffs with heavy, industrial beats. The guys are quite stoic on stage, playing simple but effective notes, while Eddie dances around like a combination of Ian Curtis and Iggy Pop. He's borderline spastic but oozes sex appeal, and he knows it.

"Fuck, that was great," says Ian when they finish. "Are you on a label?"

"No," says Eddie. "We've had some interest but nothing serious. We have a demo that we're shopping around. Jim Diamond recorded it. He's a big deal in Detroit. Do you know The White Stripes?"

"No," I say.

"I do," says Ian. "I'm friends with Long Gone John who runs Sympathy for the Record Industry. He put out their album. It's great."

"Jim recorded them at his studio," says Eddie. "We're going to do some more songs with him next month, maybe combine those with this EP for an album if we can find an interested party."

"Keep me posted," says Ian. "I've been itching to put out new bands again."

"Right on," says Eddie. He walks over to the stage and grabs two CDs from a duffel bag, handing one to Ian and one to me.

"Our contact info is on the inner sleeve if you want to stay in touch."

"Thanks, man," I say.

"Thanks, Eddie," says Ian. "Really looking forward to seeing you play tonight. Come backstage after our set and we'll talk more."

As we walk away, I ask Ian if he plans on signing them.

"If they pull it off live, I think I'll offer them a deal on the spot. They're easily as good as the L.A. groups I was telling you about and it would be nice to one-up Long Gone John. He keeps telling me how great the Detroit scene is."

When the doors open, I set up the merch table. I'm joined by a skinny brunette dressed in vintage bell bottom jeans and a hippie blouse. Death Trip guitarist Eric is with her, carrying a box of CDs.

"Is it cool if Karen sets up with you? She won't take up much room."

"No problem," I say.

I introduce myself and quickly learn that Karen is Eric's fiancé.

"So how long have you been working for the label?" Karen asks.

"Only a week," I admit. "I just landed the gig. I'm literally in the process of moving from Boston to L.A. while on tour with Solarstar."

I give her the backstory. She seems surprised that I'm so happy to be out of my office job when I mention the name of the bank I used to work for.

"That's the kind of job I wish Eric had."

"It doesn't go well with rock 'n' roll."

"Nothing does," she says. "Eddie has an agenda to be bigger than Oasis. He's said that on more than one occasion. The other guys are more realistic. Being in a band may be fun when you're in your twenties but I'm finishing my master's in social work next year. After that, Eric and I are going to get married and buy a house. If he doesn't start making money from music, it needs to be a hobby. He's too old to be working at Kinkos."

We don't say much after that. The room is mostly filled when Death Trip take the stage, a good sign. I don't want Ian to sign a band without a hometown draw. Death Trip are stellar. It's been a long time since I've been floored by an unfamiliar band. The thought of getting a chance to mold them into stars or, at least, a trendy buzz band featured in magazines like *Magnet*, *Big Takeover*, and *Alternative Press* excites me. I cross my fingers that Ian will sign them, that he'll offer me a job. I can't wait to get to L.A. and start a new life.

My wishes turn true. About fifteen minutes after Death Trip finish, Eric and Eddie greet us at the merch booth. They can barely contain themselves.

"We just got offered a record deal," blurts out Eric.

Sweat-drenched Eddie hugs me. Karen looks like she learned her puppy died.

"You could at least pretend to be happy for me," says Eric.

"I am," she says, "but it's so sudden. You only just met these guys. You barely know them. No offense to you, Drew."

"None taken," I say.

"You're going to need to hire a lawyer to look over the contract," says Karen.

"Whatever," says Eddie. "It's fucking Cherry Smash Records. Mark from Solarstar said he would help with the album. He's got a studio in Hollywood. This is everything I've ever wanted."

Eric looks uncomfortable. Karen asks if he can give her a ride home.

"You're supposed to be selling CDs," says Eric.

"While you guys drink beers backstage with your new best friends," says Karen.

"Fuck this shit," says Eddie. "Take her home, Eric. I'll hang with Drew. We need to talk business. Drew's our PR guy."

News to me, but now I know I have a job.

"Fuck, that was weird," I say to Eddie.

"Tell me about it. Karen's like fucking Yoko Ono at times. She's from Bloomfield Hills. She's a rich bitch, who pretends to be down with the out crowd. Jarvis Cocker must have known a chick like that when he wrote *Common People*."

"My ex-wife got that way after a few years. She used to love going to shows and then she went to grad school and ended up leaving me."

"Well, I'm sure you're better off without her. Eric's going to throw away his life if he marries that cunt."

"Whoa, you're not mincing your words there."

"I don't mean to be an asshole but, man, Eric is the best guitarist in Detroit. At least he is to me. He's vital to our sound."

"I can't argue with that," I say. "Think Karen will mellow out? I wouldn't want Ian to catch wind of any friction."

"There won't be. Please, don't say anything about what went down."

"I won't."

I try to lighten the mood by asking about their drummer.

"So, his name is Chinaski as in the Charles Bukowski character?"

"Yeah. That's his real name. It's not a nickname."

"So, what's his Christian name?"

"Dude, I don't even know. I think it's Steve or Scott. He was the last guy to join the band. We were auditioning drummers and he was like, I'm Chinaski. He's a strange cat but he can pound the shit out of the skins."

"Man, that's hysterical."

"That's not even the half of it. I went to his apartment once. He rents this little room off Cass. That area is a total war zone, but you know that since you're from here. He has this crappy fold-out couch that he sleeps on and this velvet painting on the wall of a flying unicorn with Pegasus wings. There's a rainbow in the background."

I can't stop laughing.

"And get this... His entire music collection is our Death Trip demo and *Appetite for Destruction*. He stores them on this huge, empty CD tower."

"Oh man, that's one of the funniest stories I've ever heard."

"He's a character, all right, but, dude, he's loyal as shit. He loves to drum, and he loves the band. We won't let you down, I promise."

Solarstar appear on stage to a chorus of cheers, immediately tearing into *Uppers and Downers*. It's the same set as always but it still feels as exciting as the first night in Boston. Eddie is mesmerized.

"Man, Mark is so cool on stage. It's all so effortless for him. I need to take notes. I get too spastic."

"You'll find your stride. You're off to a great start. Ian's been in the biz since the sixties. He's seen it all."

"That's what I'm counting on."

When the room empties, Eddie and I pack up the merch and go backstage. The Death Trip guys are hitting the beers hard, shooting the shit with Tommy, Skip, Mark, and Ian. Vic is in the corner, smoking a rollup. I join him and take a drag.

Vic says, "Here I am, on the road again."

I get the joke and respond, "And there I go, turn the page."

The Girl with the Tammy Wynette Tattoo

The next night we play Chicago, which goes off without a hitch, other than Tommy getting food poisoning after eating a post-gig tofu dog.

"Serves you right for not eating real food, Granola," says Ian after we pull over for the third time in less than an hour. "You should have had the classic Chicago dog with the bright green relish like the rest of us. At this rate, it will take us a bloody week to get to Nashville."

"Fuck you, Ian. You'll be lucky to reach sixty with all those garbage British meat pies you eat at the Cat & Fiddle."

"Yet, here I am feeling fit as a *fiddle* while you've been on the verge of shitting your pants all morning."

We all laugh. Tommy tells us to fuck off as he makes a mad dash for the toilet. Ian does have a point. The van smells like skunky beer farts and everyone is moody as fuck. Eventually, Granola's stomach settles down and we arrive at our hotel on Broadway, Nashville's main drag. With no gig tonight, everyone is anxious to cut loose.

"Has anyone gotten laid on this bloody tour yet?" asks Ian.

"Not me," says Tommy. "I've got a girlfriend."

"Ditto," says Skip.

Mark, Vic, and I also confirm in the negative. The three of us are dealing with breakup baggage.

"Christ, what's wrong with you lot?" says Ian.

"Well, what about you, Ian?" says Mark. "You've been shut down a good half-dozen times in the last week. You're losing your touch, old man."

Ian blushes. "I plan on rectifying that tonight with a nice southern belle."

"More like a jailbait Dixie skank with daddy issues," quips Tommy.

"She can call me daddy all night, Granola, as long as I get my rocks off."

We walk down Broadway, an avenue littered with neon signs, before entering one of the many honky-tonk joints. Mark's been here before and says this one caters more to locals than the sequin and denim-clad tourists, an authentic rockabilly cover band playing most nights. His words are true to form. As we enter the bar, the house band is playing the old Tiny Bradshaw classic *Train Kept A-Rollin*, later popularized by The Yardbirds. The band look the part, sporting stiff dark jeans with high turn-ups, western shirts, pompadour haircuts, and stylish sideburns.

We get strange looks from some of the regulars as we find a table in the back corner. Most of us are wearing jeans, dark T-shirts, and black leather jackets, except for Ian, who is rocking his ever-present velvet blazer and a colorful mod dress shirt.

"Y'all in a band?" asks our waitress. She appears to be in her early twenties with medium length black hair and a curvy, sexy body. A modern-day Vargas girl. She's wearing a sleeveless black top, exposing an immaculately inked tattoo of Tammy Wynette on her right arm, the words 'stand by your man' written below in cursive.

"Yeah," says Skip. "We're called Solarstar. We're from Los Angeles. We've got a gig here tomorrow night if you want to check us out."

"I'd be happy to put you on the guest list," says Ian, who's practically drooling.

"Not sure if you'd be my cup of tea, but y'all seem like nice guys, so maybe."

"What's your name?" asks Ian.

"Rose," she says.

"As in Roseanne, like Roseanne Cash?" I ask.

She smiles. "Yes. My daddy is a huge Johnny Cash fan. I do a little singing myself."

"Do you like *Jolene*?" asks Mark.

"Love it," she says. "Why do you ask?"

Mark explains the Solarstar concept of the encore covers set.

"We're going to do *I Walk the Line* and *Jolene* tomorrow, but I'd much rather have a woman sing *Jolene*. Are you interested?"

"Uh, sure!" she says.

"We're going to soundcheck tomorrow afternoon if that works," says Ian. "We're playing at Exit/In. Do you know it?"

"Yeah," she says. "It's a nice little club. A lot of touring bands play there. You'll fit in."

Rose takes our orders. The guys all get beers except for Vic, who asks for a coffee, and Mark and I, who opt for club sodas. Rose jokes about the 50/50 alcohol/non-alcohol split.

"It's more of a drinker-versus-stoner thing," says Vic.

"Y'all holding?" asks Rose.

"Always," says Mark. "We'll be here until closing if you want a hit after your shift."

"I'll take you up on that," she says.

Later, we're visited by a couple of rockabilly guys, who turn out to be German tourists paying homage to Nashville and Memphis, amongst other famous music cities. Oddly, they're both named Kristoff, but they're easy to tell apart. One of them is short and slim, the other quite heavyset. Fred and Barney, if you will.

They're in a generous mood and buy us a round of drinks.

Fred and Barney seem surprised that half of us don't drink, so Fred says to Tommy, "If your friends aren't drinking, you and Skip must join us for shots to balance out all that's good in the universe."

Skip and Tommy follow their new German friends to the bar.

"Krauts are odd as fuck," says Ian when the Germans are out of earshot.

I tell them my Fred and Barney joke and we have a good laugh. Vic says he's tired and going back to the hotel. Ian says he'll walk with him and try to 'pull' at the hotel bar. "More my scene," he says.

"Y'all the last two standing?" asks Rose when she stops by with refills.

"Looks that way," I say. "Ian and Vic went back to the hotel and I haven't seen Tommy and Skip for a while. Are they still here?"

"I'm not sure," Rose says. "One of our bartenders walked in on them and the German fellas doing blow in the men's room and I haven't seen them since. Those Germans are quite the pair. We're calling them Abbott and Costello."

"We've been calling them Fred and Barney," I say.

Rose laughs. I go on to tell her about the other nicknames in our entourage. She especially likes the Count.

"That suits him," says Rose. "Ian seems kind of smarmy, if you don't mind me saying so."

"No offense taken," says Mark, who suddenly seems aloof. "I've known him for years. He's a great boss but he's a tad creepy with the ladies."

Mark excuses himself.

"Is he okay?" Rose asks.

"I think so. Mark's a little sensitive about cocaine. He was in rehab a few years ago. That's how we know each other."

"Sorry, I didn't mean to upset him, or you for that matter."

"It's okay. Alcohol was my vice and it's not like Mark and I are Mormons. We both like to get high."

"Amen to that," she says.

I ask Rose about her tattoo. "So, who's the lucky guy?"

"What do you mean?" she asks.

"Must be a pretty special guy to deserve a 'stand by your man' tattoo."

"No one," she says. "It's wishful thinking. Old-fashioned faith, I suppose. I love Tammy Wynette and someday, just maybe, I'll meet someone worthy of that tattoo."

"Ah, the old *Field of Dreams* thing. Build it and he will come."

"You're very funny, Drew. I never did ask what instrument you played."

"I'm the publicist," I say, before giving her the Cliff's Notes version of the past few weeks.

"Wow, that's quite a story. I've never been to Los Angeles."

"First time for me, too. I need a change. Boston reminds me too much of my ex. I need a fresh start."

"I've got my share of exes but most of them are still here. I can't run away like you. This is where I need to be to make it in music."

Rose heads back to the bar. When Mark returns he hands me a baggy with two freshly rolled joints.

"I'm going back to the hotel, but this is for you and Rose. She likes you. I don't want to be a cockblocker. Just make sure she gets you to the club by soundcheck if you get lucky."

"Where's Mark?" Rose asks when she stops by to tell me it's last call.

"He went back to the hotel, but he left me a little something if you're still interested."

I show her the baggie.

"I'm most definitely interested," Rose says. "Want to come back to my place? My shift is about to end, and I don't have to close tonight."

"Sure."

Rose lives in a small apartment, not far from the bar. The furniture is old-fashioned, like it could have belonged to her grandparents. There are framed posters of country music icons in the living room and several crates of albums next to a vintage stereo console. She puts on an old Byrds album.

"I'm guessing The Byrds are good common ground for us," laughs Rose.

"I love The Byrds. Great choice."

She pours herself a glass of bourbon and brings me a soda. I light up a joint and offer her a drag. She takes a long hit and hands it back to me. I'm not sure where this is leading but I'm feeling loose and relaxed.

"So, what's your story, Drew? Got any ex-wives and kids?"

"One ex-wife, no kids. I'm very single now."

I tell her about Emily and my not so happy years in Boston.

"I'm in a similar boat myself," says Rose. "My ex-boyfriend Clint left me for another woman six months ago. They're living in Austin now."

"Musician?" I ask.

"Yup. Musician and a Grade-A asshole."

"To moving on," I say.

We clink glasses and she kisses me softly before leading me to the bedroom. I get aroused watching her sexy ass sway in her short denim skirt. We undress before she sits down on the bed to remove her cowboy boots.

"Keep them on," I say. "They look really hot."

"Got a shoe fetish?" she teases.

"I have a soft spot for boots and heels," I admit.

She grabs a cowboy hat from her dresser and models it for me.

"How about I give you the full Nashville treatment, then?"

Afterwards we lay back in bed and pass around the second joint.

"I like you a lot, Drew. If you're ever back in town, you know where to find me."

"I might not. You could be famous by then."

She smiles. "If I am, you can be on my guest list for life. If I ever make it out to Hollywood, you'll have to show me that Sunset Trip."

I laugh and say, "You mean Strip. Sunset Strip."

"Oh my god, I'm so high," she giggles. "Sunset Trip! Well, if I smoke any more of this stuff, it's going to feel like I'm on a permanent Sunset Trip."

"Normally, Mark mixes it with tobacco. It's been a while since I've been this stoned."

"Want some pancakes? I always get the munchies for breakfast food when I'm high."

Roses makes an amazing batch of chocolate chip pancakes, which I barely remember eating. It's just after noon when we wake up. She makes a strong pot of coffee, which we nurse until it's time to go to the Exit/In for soundcheck.

When we arrive, the band are setting up. Mark greets us with a copy of *Alternative Press*.

"Hot off the presses. I bought it at a newsstand this morning. Your Solarstar feature turned out great. Did I really say all that shit?"

"You sure did. Rob has the taped evidence."

Mark flips open the magazine to the appropriate spot, proudly showing it to me and Rose. Rose squeezes my hand.

"I didn't know you were a writer, Drew."

"He's a man of many talents," says Mark.

"I can attest to that," says Rose.

Some of the guys chuckle.

"I'm guessing none of you got laid last night," Rose retorts. Most of them blush.

"I met a nice lady at the hotel bar," says Ian, "but I don't kiss and tell."

"Bullshit," says Tommy. "That's all you ever do."

"Well, fuck you, Granola," says Ian, who has turned beet red. "I'm surprised you and Skip are even alive after doing blow with those Kraut fucks all night."

"I'll survive," says Skip before excusing himself. "I think I have to throw up again."

When Skip returns, the band finishes setting up. Rose nails *Jolene* on the first take.

"That was perfect," says Mark.

"Well, thank you. You guys sure can play. I didn't know what to expect. What time should I meet y'all tonight?"

"Swing by around eight. I'll have the door guy take you backstage," says Ian.

Before leaving, Rose gives me a long kiss in front of the other guys. "See you tonight, Drew."

"See you soon."

"Fuck, Drew, you've turned out to be a real dark horse," says Ian after Rose leaves the building.

"What the fuck is dark horse?" asks Tommy.

"Someone who's secretive," says Ian. "You know, someone who has a bit more up his sleeve than one might suspect."

"Dark horse. I love it," says Tommy. "Looks like everyone has a nickname now."

"What about Mark?" asks Vic.

"Mark's too cool to have a nickname," says Tommy. "He's the man with no name."

"Well, that counts," says Skip. "Mark can be Eastwood, the man with no name."

He'll always be Dr. Rock to me, but I keep my trap shut.

"So, what about me, then?" asks Ian.

Everyone laughs before Vic says, "Nothing yet, Ian, but we'll find something suitable for you. You can *count* on it."

Interview with the Vampire

The Exit/In gig has been oversold and, at times, I can barely move, even within the confines of the merch booth. I'm selling more than usual. When I get backstage, I let Ian know our stock is low and he makes a note in his diary to phone Danny Scorpio at the office in the morning to have more goods shipped to the venue in New Orleans. We have just enough for Memphis tomorrow.

Rose is ecstatic. She nailed *Jolene* and has been buzzing for a good half-hour since the band left the stage.

"If I ever get a record deal, can I hire you guys to be my band?" she keeps asking.

"Sure," says Tommy, who tells her about Catalina Coast. "You'd like us. We're way into stuff like the Flying Burrito Brothers, Gram Parsons, and The Byrds."

"You're speaking my language."

"There's a great country scene in L.A.," adds Vic. "I'm sure Drew wouldn't mind if you came out for a visit."

He pokes me in the ribs and I blush a little.

"Speaking of, is it okay if I borrow Drew for another night?" Rose asks.

"Fine," says Ian, "but we're making an early start for Memphis. We've booked visits to Graceland and the old Sun Records studios."

"I won't kidnap Drew, then. I wouldn't want him to miss out on his history lessons."

When we get to her place, Rose and I talk for hours.

"If I never see you again, Drew, thanks for brightening up my life these past few days."

"Ditto."

"Life's not like the movies," she says. "If this were a movie, you'd stay here, or I'd run away with you to Los Angeles, but Nashville isn't for you, Drew. I can tell. All the signs are pointing for you to head west."

I reluctantly agree.

"I'm too much of a southern girl. Nashville's home."

"I'll miss you."

"Doesn't mean our little movie can't have a happy ending, if you catch my drift."

She kisses me before we make love for the last time.

*

I'm surprised at how unassuming Graceland is. It's downright modest next to the opulent mansions Robin Leach used to flaunt on *Lifestyles of the Rich and Famous*. A few of the guys buy disposable cameras at a local pharmacy and we ham it up in front of the famous Jungle Room, which features an indoor waterfall and an assortment of tropical-themed furnishings, including a collection of ceramic monkeys. After, we take a short drive to the Sun studio, located in a desolate section of the city. It blows my mind that the room is so small, that so much magic was created in such a tiny space. When we stop at a gas station to fill up the van, I buy a black coffee mug with the iconic Sun logo.

Danny Scorpio rings Ian as we're driving to the club for soundcheck. From what I can gather, the merch is on its way to New Orleans, but Danny has more news. Ian keeps saying things like "holy shit" and "you're fucking kidding, mate." Before hanging up he says, "Mark's going to be angry."

"Angry at what?" says Mark.

"Matthew fucking St. James," says Ian. "He's recorded a new version of *Bullet* for his next album. They want to release it as a single next month. The label is convinced it will be a contender for the Christmas number one."

Having the number one single at Christmas is a big deal in the UK.

"I don't give a fuck," says Mark, "as long as I get the royalties. I wrote the fucking song."

"Well, technically it's a 50/50 split," says Ian, "since Matthew re-did the guitar parts."

"Whatever," says Mark. "If it charts, I can pay off my fucking mortgage, live a little."

Mark is off his game in Memphis. Nothing that anyone in the crowd would notice but, having seen them a good half-dozen times, I can tell that he's not feeling it. Before playing the set finale *Bullet*, Mark makes a dig at Matthew for choosing to cover Solarstar's most beloved song. The encore is better when Mark gets out of his skin and the band rip the joint on Big Star's *September Gurls* and Chris Bell's swirling psychedelic *I am the Cosmos*.

We get a day off in New Orleans, where Solarstar played their infamous final gig. The guys are motivated to lift the curse.

"Do I need to hire a fucking witch doctor?" jokes Ian.

Mark invites me to Lafayette Cemetery in the Lower Garden District. He's getting interviewed by a local entertainment magazine and Mark wants to conduct it there because the cemetery is featured in his favorite novel *Interview with the Vampire*.

"I know I'm goth as fuck," admits Mark as we take a streetcar down St. Charles, a boulevard which runs from the French Quarter into a more prosperous tree-lined residential area.

"This whole city is goth as fuck," I say. "I know I've only been here for a few hours but there's something dark and creepy about this place, yet I can't help but love it."

"We spent a few days here in '88, waiting for updates about Matthew from that fucking detective. Bobby and Chris went on benders in the Quarter, but I got to know the city. I took a lot of long walks and made friends with one of our fans, who took me to some cool record stores and the less touristy places. Have you read *Interview*?"

"Yeah, but I saw the movie first. I know, I'm lame, but I do like the novel better."

"Kristi bought me a copy for my sixteenth birthday. It was one of her favorite books."

"I had no idea it was that old."

"Yeah, it came out in '76. It took Anne Rice a long time to get the credit she deserved. I can relate to that. I don't want to be famous when dead. The thought of that keeps me awake at night."

The cemetery is in a beautiful magnolia-shaded park with rows of stone tombs as far as the eye can see. I feel like I'm eavesdropping on remnants from an alien civilization, the tombs so different in structure to traditional American gravestones.

The girl interviewing Mark is nice. It's almost November, but the temperatures are still pushing eighty, even in the shade. I'm in jeans and a T-shirt, but Mark and the scribe are sporting black leather jackets like true rock 'n' roll vampires. Mark tells the journalist why he chose the location. She asks why he likes the novel so much.

"I always loved the book, but when Solarstar broke up the story took on a whole new meaning. I completely relate to Louis, the reclusive vampire with a heart.

Matthew turned out to be Lestat, the star-struck asshole."

"I hear that he's going to cover *Bullet*. How do you feel about that?"

"At first, I was pissed off, but it's just a song. I'm proud that Matthew thinks that something I wrote is better than anything he can come up with. Good songs are timeless, so I suppose I need to let it go."

When the interview commences, Mark asks the journalist if she's going to the show. She admits that she doesn't have a ticket, that it's sold out. He takes her name and promises to put her on the guest list. When she leaves, I tell Mark that was a nice thing to do.

"Just a small favor for a new friend. I need to even up my scorecard before I meet my maker."

"I can relate. Do you believe in God?"

"That's a little deep, Drew, but, no, I don't. I do believe that there's something more out there, though."

"I'm with you. I was technically dead for a few minutes. I knew who I was, but it felt like a TV channel had been changed on me."

"This conversation has certainly turned heavy in a hurry, Drew. Anyway, it takes strength to be gentle and kind."

"Okay, Morrissey."

"Ha! I knew I couldn't slip that by you, but I tried."

We laugh before Mark hugs me. It feels awkward and unexpected, like he's saying goodbye.

We take a quick walk around the cemetery. I take a few photos and we briefly join a tour group, catching snippets of local history from an enthusiastic guide. It's a welcome escape from endless hours in the van, staring out at ugly farmland; the monotonous journey only broken by piss breaks at filthy rest stops and meals at craptastic fast food chains. The low-budget motels we crash at each evening feel like paradise after a typical day on the road.

Scorpio Rising

There's a song called *Polaroids* by Kitchens of Distinction, an underrated English group, who had a decent run in the late eighties and early nineties. It's a nostalgic account of faded, foggy memories kept alive by old photographs. They could have been writing about my experiences on the second half of the Solarstar tour. The cities, venues, hotels, and people we befriended became a blur as we made our way west to Los Angeles via Austin, Denver, Salt Lake City, Portland, Seattle, and San Francisco. These days, when I pull out the photos, certain memories return in vivid color. A group of lapsed Mormon girls, posing in front of the Tabernacle after they scored us weed; a snapshot Ian took of me and Mark with The Dandy Warhols at their favorite Portland dive; one of me and Vic, lost in thought, sipping tea at a café in San Francisco's Chinatown.

We arrive in Los Angeles on a Wednesday afternoon, the week before Thanksgiving. Mark and I get dropped off at his place. Hollywood is far more residential and suburban than I expected, at least this section of town. Mark's street is a combination of apartment complexes and bungalows. I pause after we place our belongings on the curbside.

"Are you okay?" asks Mark.

"Yeah. I've never seen a palm tree in real life, just savoring the moment."

"I think you're the first person who's ever been impressed with Detroit Street."

"Just a midwestern boy, soaking it all up."

"Let's get this shit inside," Mark says. "The neighborhood is safe, but I don't want people noticing that I own expensive gear."

Mark's bungalow is sparse with hardwood floors. The largest bedroom has been converted into a recording studio. It's a tight space, but Mark tells me there's enough room to fit a full drum kit, when necessary. He gives me an equipment tutorial, which is mostly Greek to me. I've been in recording studios a few times but those of the more old-fashioned variety with gigantic soundboards. Mark explains that the old-school studio is a dying breed, that one can record just as well with a minimalist set-up.

"With Pro-Tools, I can record up to twenty-four tracks and I don't have to pay a fortune to some fat slob with a ponytail to twiddle the knobs."

Mark shows me the guest room, where I'm to crash. It's about the size of a Japanese hotel room, with a fold out futon.

"Hope it's not too cramped," Mark says.

"Nah, I'm fine. I like to live econo."

"Nice Minutemen reference. Mike Watt is a cool cat. Have you met him?"

"No. I was never a huge fan, to be honest, but I liked their simple approach to life."

"Glad we agree there. I'd kick you out if you were a hoarder."

"No worries. I don't own much. If it's okay with you, I'm going to have my brother ship a box of records. That's all I own right now, besides the clothes in my suitcase."

Mark shows me the living room. There's a small couch, coffee table, no television, and a stereo console with a turntable and an assortment of high-end components. His collection is smaller than I would have expected, just single shelves for his LPs and CDs.

As if anticipating my question, Mark says, "I tend to play the same fifty records repeatedly. People keep giving me CDs, but I sell them at Aron's. They're the best record store on this side of town. It's walking distance from here, though people in this town always freak out when I tell them I like to walk. Most people will spend twenty minutes looking for a parking space when they could have walked to their destination in half the time."

"I like to walk. I did a lot of that in Boston, though we had a great subway system, too."

"Los Angeles has a subway, as well."

"No shit?"

"Yeah, but the stops are in weird and random locations. I guess they made more sense back in the day. Look, if you want to hit the shower first, I'll do a load of laundry. That's the first thing I do when I come back from tour. I need to decompress and wash away the scum."

I sleep until noon. When I get dressed, I walk into the living room where Mark is seated on a chair getting his hair cut by a brunette with sleeve tattoos.

"Morning, sleepy head," says Mark. "This is Kim. You're next up if you want a haircut."

"Sure," I say.

After six weeks of touring my hair has finally grown past my ears – the Boston businessman look nothing more than a bad memory – but I could use a trim.

"How much do I owe you?" I ask Kim.

"Mark's got that covered," she says. "He won't drive to my salon in Beverly Hills, so he pays me extra to come here. It's like that movie *Shampoo*, but without the extra perks if you catch my drift."

"I don't like to leave my grid," laughs Mark.

"For a rock star, you're such a homebody," says Kim as she applies a finishing touch of hairspray. "You have such nice hair, Mark, but I wish you wouldn't use so much product. That's so eighties."

"It's his trademark," I say.

When it's my turn, Kim doesn't do much, other than thinning it out and giving it some shape. I always tell stylists to use mid-sixties Keith Richards as a reference point and she does a good job.

"Give it a few weeks and it will be your ideal length," she says.

When Kim leaves, Mark and I walk to the Cherry Smash offices. On the way, we cross La Brea, a main drag full of shops and restaurants. Mark points out Pink's, a world-famous hot dog stand, which has a line around the corner, even at this early mid-morning hour.

"Tourists always go to Pink's," says Mark. "It's not that good but I suppose I should take you there sometime just for the experience."

"As long as they don't have tofu dogs. I don't want to get the shits like Granola did in Chicago."

Cherry Smash is next door to a trendy coffee shop. We stop there and buy four cups to go. I'm excited to meet the mysterious Danny Scorpio. I wonder if it's his real name. I learn it's not when I'm introduced.

"Just something I use when I write for magazines," says Danny. "My birthday's in November, so there you go."

Danny looks like a surfer with his long blonde hair and three-day stubble.

Ian has his own office. Mark joins him there while Danny shows me our space, a slightly larger room with two desks. There are several filing cabinets, where we keep contracts and tax-related paperwork, and a beaten-up couch.

"We used to have an intern, but she sucked, so Ian had to fire her before the tour. This is your desk now," he says, pointing to a freshly polished workspace opposite Danny's. The office walls are decorated with concert posters and flyers of sixties garage and seventies punk rock acts.

"Ian's stuck in that whole '66/'77 aesthetic," says Danny. "I'm glad that he finally listened to me and wants to put out new bands. He mailed me the Death Trip demo. Great shit. They remind me of Black Rebel Motorcycle Club."

"That's what I keep hearing, but I've yet to hear them."

Danny takes a CD off his desk. "This is a self-released album that B.R.M.C. put out. It landed them a deal with Virgin Records. They're going to be huge. I can tell. They're supporting Solarstar tomorrow night."

Mark pops the CD into a large boombox and we sit down on the couch and take in the sounds. I immediately dig it. They're heavy and melodic, like a Mary Chain for the new century.

"Nice," I say.

"Right on. I assumed you'd dig it. I'll give you a full rundown of our database and mail order system tomorrow. You'll pick it up right away. You don't need to be a rocket scientist to work for a record label. I tend to focus on the reissue projects; tracking down the artists, getting licensing permits, all the legal bullshit. Ian's going to get you started on the Death Trip album. He wants to release it in June."

"That far away?" I ask.

"Yeah, there's a lot to be done. Eddie called the other day and said they recorded five new songs. Mark's going to combine the two EPs into an album, shuffle the song order a bit, and master it. Ian wants to release a seven-inch first as a teaser to whet the music press' appetite. It's all a hype game, man. Get the product in the right people's hands and let the magic happen."

I listen intently. I've been writing about music my entire adult life, but this is a side of the business I know next to nothing about.

"So, when's the last time you had a good meal?" Danny asks.

"Fuck, probably when my ex-girlfriend moved out over a year ago."

"You're not a vegetarian or anything, are you?"

"Hell, no. I would have already told you if I was! I did feel bad for Tommy on tour, though. The guys kept calling him Granola."

"I like it. Lots of the kids in the scene think they're Laurel Canyon hippies from the sixties with their beansprouts and bongs. Like steak?"

"Yeah."

"Right on. I'll take you to the Bounty. You'll love it. Then we'll hit Three Clubs. Beachwood Sparks are playing tonight. Do you know them?"

"Not personally, but I have the *Desert Skies* single. It's great."

"They're fantastic live," says Danny. "We'll have a good time. Three Clubs is where everyone hangs out on Thursdays. There's always a good band or DJ. I go there a lot on Sundays, too. No bands but it's a more mellow vibe. You can actually hear the people you're having conversations with."

Danny picks me up in the early evening. He looks sharp in a vintage western shirt, jeans, and Clark's Wallabees. I'm wearing black jeans, a long sleeve black T-shirt, and black boots and immediately worry that I'll look out of place. I tell Danny and he laughs.

"You're cool, man. You're dressed like the guys in B.R.M.C. and The Warlocks. Three Clubs is an inclusive scene. You'll see people representing every rock 'n' roll subculture, except metal dudes. Ever see the movie *Swingers*?"

"Yeah."

"Those goofasaurus types used to hang out at Three Clubs when the swing scene was happening, but the bar is more rock 'n' roll these days, at least the nights I'm there."

Danny has a nice car, an early eighties El Dorado.

"Sweet ride," I tell him.

"Thanks, man. The gas mileage sucks and it's a pain in the ass to park, but it would break my heart to part ways with her. You'll need to get some wheels soon, yourself. This is a big fucking city. Maybe Mark will let you borrow his until then."

"What does Mark drive? He made it sound like he walks everywhere."

"He definitely stays in his little grid, but he has a badass Cadillac convertible. Late seventies model, fully restored."

"I had no idea."

"He's a mysterious dude."

Danny points out a few sights on our drive, including the La Brea Tar Pits. When I was a kid, I was fascinated with prehistoric mammals, like mammoths and sabre tooth tigers. I make a mental note to visit sometime.

The Bounty is on Wilshire in Koreatown, halfway between Hollywood and Downtown. The restaurant is a total retro throwback with leather booths, dim red lighting, and tacky nautical décor.

"It's a dive but the steaks are decent," says Danny, "and I like the vibe. I hate everything in this city west of Fairfax, except for a few clubs, like the Troubadour."

"You don't strike me as a Sunset Strip dude."

"Nah, that was never my scene. There are some hot girls who hang out at the Rainbow if you're into slutty metal girls in spandex."

"I tend to fall for the mod types."

"Plenty of that at Three Clubs, plus there are some good club nights for the more hardcore types, the ones who pretend they've time traveled from Carnaby Street."

"Like Ian?"

"Yeah. He's a bit of a fop, but he's a good boss. I could be making more at a larger label, but Cherry Smash is a mellow ride."

"How long have you been working there?"

"Three years. I was working at Aron's Records before that. I like working for a label better than retail, I can tell you that much. What have you done besides writing?"

"A few soul-sucking office jobs here and there. I don't seem to have the fortitude for that lifestyle."

We arrive at Three Clubs just after ten.

"Usually it doesn't fill up until closer to midnight," Danny says, "but this way I can introduce you to a few people before it gets loud and crazy."

Three Clubs is in a strip mall on the corner of Santa Monica and Vine in Hollywood. There's no identifier, just a gaudy yellow sign above the building, which says, "Bargain Clown Mart."

The bar is dark with black booths and dim red lighting. I'm sensing a theme, though the décor here is far more tasteful than the Bounty. There are two rooms. The smaller space, where we enter, has a large semi-circular bar. There's a larger room to the right, where the bands play. Danny and I grab a couple of stools at the bar. He introduces me to Tami, a stylish brunette who books the bands and DJs. She pours Danny a Jack and Coke and asks what I'll have. I order a club soda and lime.

"Drew just started at Cherry Smash," says Danny. "He moved here from Boston."

"Welcome," says Tami. "Where are you living?"

"I'm crashing with Mark Jennings in Hollywood for now," I say.

"Mark's a great guy. Tell him to stop by sometime. I keep trying to get him to play here."

"He can be reclusive," I say.

"You don't say," laughs Danny.

"Well, tell him I said hey," says Tami.

"Will do. He's been working on new songs, I'd like to hear them myself."

Danny and I make the rounds, drinks in hand. I'm having a hard time keeping up with all the new names and faces. It feels like I'm in a hipster version of *The Warriors*, with so many different music subcultures represented. It's like what Danny said earlier, a mix of mods, rockers dressed in black, and friends and fans of the Beachwood Sparks sporting the Laurel Canyon country rock look.

I run into Tommy and Skip, who are talking to Brent from Beachwood Sparks and his brother Darren, who Danny later tells me fronts a group called The Tyde.

"Long time, Drew," laughs Tommy.

"Yeah, it's been years. How are you guys?"

I keep getting offered drinks and begin to feel uncomfortable. The combination of an increasingly crowded room and the presence of too much alcohol is making me uneasy, like it did a few times on tour. I tell Danny I'm going outside for air. A few people are smoking in the parking lot. I lean up against a wall and spark up a funny cigarette. I take a few hits and try to relax. I forgot to take my Valium today, which also reminds me that I'm almost out and that I need to find a new doctor. I'm panicking and want to find a payphone to call Mark, see if he can pick me up.

I'm within earshot of a loud group of girls. One of them approaches me. She's blonde and beautiful, a little on the thin side. She looks like someone I should know, like she's a model or an actress. She asks if she can bum a cigarette. I tell her I don't have any but offer her a hit from my joint.

"It's half tobacco and half weed, if you don't mind."

"That's fine," she says, before taking a long drag. "I've been trying to quit anyway. This will take the edge off. Thanks."

"You're welcome."

Before I can introduce myself, her friends call her back.

"Later," she says with a smile.

"I hope so," I say.

"So, who was the chick, Drew? Did you get her number?"

It's Danny.

"I didn't get a chance. Her friends dragged her off, just as we were starting to talk. Do you know her?"

"No, but I've seen her around."

"I feel like I know her from somewhere, like she's a model or an actress."

"She probably is. Lots of minor celebrities like to slum it here. Seth Green and Parker Posey stop by sometimes but, hey, Beachwood Sparks are about to come on. You don't want to miss them."

We go inside. Danny and I find a vantage point in the back where we have some breathing space. I haven't felt this off since that day I interviewed Mark in Cleveland. Hopefully the weed will kick in. Danny points out Anton Newcombe, who is in the back of the room, pouring a tall can of Boddingtons into a pint glass.

"He looks approachable today," says Danny. "Sometimes he goes off on these manic jags."

We walk over and say hi. Anton's wearing a Levi's corduroy jacket with matching jeans, his long shaggy hair partially covering his face as if he were trying to avoid being recognized. I remind Anton that we met at a BJM show in Boston a few years ago.

"I remember you," he says in a slight surfer dude drawl. "Are you in Los Angeles for good?

"I think so."

"Be careful what you wish for," he says.

I laugh, not knowing how to take it.

"So how are things?" I ask. "Tommy and Skip told me that you're working on new songs. I can't wait to hear them."

"You'll like them," he says. "You guys should come by my place sometime and listen to them, maybe do a story for *Left Coast Underground*."

"That would be cool," says Danny.

"But let's keep it to the music, okay? No one seems to want to talk about my art anymore. People come to shows to heckle me or see a fight. I'm sick of getting asked about guns and drugs."

Anton has an intense bug-eyed expression. He takes a sip from his pint as he gathers his thoughts.

"The new album is going to be a real rock 'n' roll record. That's what the world needs right now, you know."

A girl bumps into Anton before he can continue, spilling some of her drink on to his shirt. He yells at her before storming off. Danny laughs.

"Welcome to Los Angeles."

Punk Rock Girl

I spend the next day with Danny, learning the ropes at Cherry Smash. Ian takes the day off to help with pre-gig logistics. I'm off merch duty. Skip's girlfriend's stint on *Dawson's Creek* has come to an end, and she's going to run the booth.

Danny takes me to a sushi joint before we head to the show at the Troubadour, which borders Hollywood and Beverly Hills. There's a huge line outside, which we thankfully avoid; perks of being on the guest list. The club is filling fast. Black Rebel Motorcycle Club are on soon and I notice a lot of faces I saw at Three Clubs last night. There's a definite buzz about the black leather-clad outfit.

When we get backstage, Mark is pacing around the room. I can tell that he's nervous, so I leave him alone and walk over to Vic, who is sitting on a chair, tuning his guitar.

"Hey, man," he says.

"Hey, Vic. How's it going?"

"Okay, I guess, but it's weird, this being the last show and all. I feel like I finished a tour of duty in 'Nam and I'm still jonesing for action. How are you settling in?"

I tell him about my adventures at the Bounty and Three Clubs and my first day on the job.

"Hope it goes well for you," he says. "I'm moving back to San Francisco, after all. I'm going to crash with a friend until I find a job. A buddy has a new band in the works. He's a great singer and I'm going to play guitar."

"Keep me posted."

"You know I will, now that you're a record label mogul," he jokes.

B.R.M.C. tear it up, so much so that Danny wonders out loud if Solarstar will be able to top it. They're a trio but sound massive. The guitarist Peter and bass player Robert share vocal duties, while an English expat named Nick keeps beat. I notice a couple of songs from the CD Danny played me, plus one I don't recognize, a punk-fueled rocker with a chorus that questions, whatever happened to my rock 'n' roll?

Solarstar play their best gig of the tour. A few days of rest have done wonders for Mark. I could tell that he was worn out as the tour wound down, especially in San Francisco when he sucked down cough drops all day and barely spoke to anyone to save his voice. Before *Bullet*, Mark makes a joke about the forthcoming Matthew St. James cover.

"This is a song I wrote about an old girlfriend," he says, as he cradles the mic stand in a pose worthy of Dave Gahan. "I didn't get the girl, but Matthew's version will pay off my mortgage, so thanks old friend, wherever you are."

Danny and I go backstage and hang out with the guys. Most of them are raiding the cooler for celebratory beers, while Ian is doing his best to charm several pretty young things. I notice Ian Astbury and Billy Duffy from The Cult and Tim Burgess from The Charlatans making the rounds. English expats in the City of Angels. I take a seat on a large couch next to Mark, who sparks a joint. He takes a long drag and says, "Time for the rest of my life."

He passes the joint to me.

"Amen," I say.

"Pre-seventies men forever," laughs Mark.

One of the security guys approaches us.

"There's a chick here to see you, Mark, but she doesn't have a pass."

"I didn't invite anyone," says Mark. "Did she give you a name?"

"No, she wouldn't. She was being all mysterious and shit. She said to tell you that 'it looks like it saved your life,' whatever the hell that means."

Mark turns white and nearly faints. I hold on to him until he recovers from the shock. He gasps, "Let her in."

Kristi enters the room and Mark rises to greet her. No words are exchanged. They hug for what seems like an eternity. I feel like a voyeur – Iggy Pop's passenger – observing a defining moment in Mark's life, the closure he longed for in the interview we conducted. Mark and Kristi join me on the couch. She looks fit, like she's a runner or a regular at the gym. Her hair is short and still bleached blonde, the way I imagined it looked when she was a teen. She's wearing skinny black jeans, Doc Martens, and a faded black and silver Solarstar T-shirt from the eighties. It's clear she kept tabs on Mark over the years.

There's a moment of awkward silence until Mark says, "I can't believe you remembered that line about the guitar."

"I totally forgot I said that until I read the article in *Alternative Press*. That's why I'm here."

"Drew wrote it, so I guess I owe you one, Drew," says Mark as he turns in my direction.

"You've done enough for me, already," I say. "Do you guys want me to leave?"

"No," says Mark. "I need you to stay or else I'll start to think that this is nothing more than a beautiful dream.

Kristi laughs.

"So, how long have you been in L.A.?" asks Mark.

"Two years," she says. "I had no idea you were living here until I read the article. I assumed you were still in England."

"So, what are you doing with yourself these days?" Mark asks.

"I teach creative writing at CalArts."

"Do you live out there?"

"No, I'm in Hollywood. I don't mind the commute."

"I'm in Hollywood, too. Where do you live?"

"McCadden, just off Sunset."

"I'm a bit south of you," says Mark. "I always hoped you wouldn't change, Kristi. It looks like you haven't."

"We still have the same haircuts!"

She edges closer to Mark and they lock hands.

"So, the haircut story's true?" I ask. "I thought maybe Mark was embellishing that."

"No, it's all true. I took this boy's virginity and five minutes later, he's pointing at a picture of Stiv Bators, saying 'I want that haircut!'"

"What was he like before he became a punk?"

"Hey," says Mark. "Are you writing a fucking book about me?"

Kristi laughs.

"The day I met Mark he was wearing a David Bowie T-shirt. He had long brown feathered hair. He was a total stoner boy. I had a huge crush on him. I'd see him walking in the halls, but we didn't have any classes together. It took us a week to cross paths when we met in detention. Ever see *Dazed and Confused*?"

"Yeah," I say.

"Well, Mark was like that main character, the kid who wouldn't sign the football coach's pledge. Everyone liked Mark; the popular kids, the stoners, the art geeks. Mark took it all in stride, like he didn't give a fuck. The jocks kept bugging him to join the baseball team."

"Fucking Coop," laughs Mark.

"Ha! I remember Scott Cooper," says Kristi, "and his sidekicks, Washington and Sadowski."

"Washington was okay," says Mark, "but, man, did I hate Sadowski. He was a total douchebag. His older sister was a slut. Coop, Washington and I always used to tease Sadowski about that. I stopped hanging out with those guys after my dad died, but they still liked me for some reason."

"Because you were rejecting them," says Kristi. "Most people want to be popular in high school. Guys like Coop couldn't understand why anyone wouldn't like him. Did Mark ever tell you how he broke Sadowski's nose and got kicked out of school for a week?"

"Oh fuck," says Mark. "Don't remind me."

"When Mark and I started going together, Sadowski called me a slut. I told Mark and Mark just walked up to him and punched him."

"Let's say I used to have anger issues. There's a reason why I don't drink or do coke anymore, but enough about me. You read the article, so you know how I feel, Kristi. I fucked up by never writing you back. I owe you."

"Well, I'm here now, so that's a start."

"Are you still writing?" asks Mark.

"Yes," she says. "I've had two poetry collections published, but teaching pays the bills."

"What were you doing before you came here?"

"Well, I did end up going to Oberlin and then I went to NYU. After that I got a teaching job at an art school in the city. I thought I would be in New York for life but when my boyfriend and I broke up, I started fantasizing about moving away. The job opening at CalArts came at the right time."

"So, are you single?" asks Mark.

"I am, until you ask me out."

Mark laughs and turns to me.

"I love this girl. She never minces words."

"I think I'm going to mingle," I say. "Can I bring you a beer, Kristi?"

"Sure," she says.

"Soda for me," says Mark.

I bring them their drinks. They barely notice. I join Ian, who has finished schmoozing with Ian and Billy from The Cult.

"So, back to bloody normal again, eh, Drew?"

"Yeah," I say. "The tour was fun but I'm looking forward to having a regular routine again."

"Danny likes you a lot."

"He's a cool dude."

"We'll talk more on Monday, but I can't wait to get started on Death Trip. That B.R.M.C. set was great. A year from now, it's going to be Death Trip opening for a name act. So, is that who I think it is?" asks Ian, pointing in Mark and Kristi's direction.

"Sure is."

"Well, here's to the punk rock girl and Mark's happiness. He's like the son I never had. I hope the new century will be kinder to him."

Voices Carry

Mark takes me for a drive in his shiny black Cadillac. I feel like I'm James Brown, as he chauffeurs me around town.

"I try to take her out at least once a week to keep her happy, and I get her washed and waxed every few weeks," he says, as we cruise north on LaBrea to Sunset, before turning left towards Beverly Hills.

"Never figured you for a gearhead," I say.

"My dad taught me a lot when he had the time. I know the basics. I have a trustworthy mechanic for anything complicated. We met in rehab. The two of us brought the car back from the dead. I'm sure there's a metaphor there."

Mark points out the famous rock 'n' roll landmarks on Sunset. The Viper Room, where River Phoenix snuffed it and Mark played that infamous solo gig; the Rainbow, where Lemmy from Motörhead can be found on slot machines when he's not touring, Jack and Coke in hand; and the Whisky a Go Go, where The Doors and, later, metal acts like Mötley Crüe, Poison, and Guns N' Roses honed their chops.

"The Whisky used to be cool," says Mark, "but now it's just pay-to-play bullshit. I figured I'd show you the Strip this one time, but if you ever want to come back, that's on you."

He can't stop talking about Kristi. They're going out to dinner tonight and he's as antsy as a high-school boy, prepping for prom.

"That was the weirdest thing," I say. "I was so sad when you told me about her in the interview."

"It's the article, Drew. If anyone else conducted that interview, I wouldn't have been so open. Now, if I could only do something for you..."

"Dude, you're giving me a free place to crash. I wouldn't have my job with Ian if it weren't for you."

"Well, I feel like I owe you and I'm going to watch out for you. I'm not going to let you fuck up like I did."

When we reach the iconic Beverly Hills sign, Mark makes a U-Turn. We have lunch plans with Ian at the Cat & Fiddle, which is on Sunset in the heart of Hollywood.

"We must be close to where Kristi lives," Mark says when we cross McCadden. "She said she lived near the corner of Sunset and McCadden."

"Easy there, you're starting to sound like a stalker."

"I know. I'm worrying about what to wear tonight and how my hair looks. I'm acting like a fucking fag."

The Cat & Fiddle is owned by Kim Gardner, who was in the cult English sixties mod band The Creation. Mark tells me that all the British expats hang out there, even the reclusive Morrissey. Ian's seated on a table in the courtyard next to a fountain when we arrive, sipping on a pint. Though it's November, the temps are in the seventies. I can get used to this.

"Welcome, gents," says Ian.

We all order fish and chips. Ian and I scarf down our portions, but Mark barely touches his plate.

"What's wrong with you, mate?" asks Ian. "Normally, you have the appetite of a bloody teenager."

"I'm nervous," he says. "I have a date with Kristi tonight."

"Whoa, moving fast there, mate. She is a tasty bird, though. A bit old for me, mind you."

"Fuck you, Ian," says Mark with a grin.

"She seems cool," I say. "Wonder if she has any single friends?"

"I can ask," says Mark.

"Make sure they're under thirty, though," I say. "Women who are my age hate me."

"You're like me, Drew," says Ian. "Always chasing the fountain of youth."

"Maybe," I say, "but it's also financial. Women in their thirties want to settle down, get married and buy a house. I'm terrible at adult shit."

"We all are," says Mark. "That's why we're in the music biz. It's a requisite that you remain immature as fuck. I'm shocked that Kristi is still cool, to be honest. I thought she would have become a suburban housewife by now, married to some executive, like her mom was."

I stay in that night. Danny Scorpio invited me to a party in Silverlake, but the last few months have caught up with me. I'm shot. I listen to a few of Mark's records before going to bed.

The next morning, I hear voices in the living room. I'm guessing Kristi spent the night. I throw on a pair of jeans and a T-shirt and head to the kitchen. I catch the tail end of something that Kristi says and stop.

"If we get as serious as I think we are, you have to promise that you'll look after Drew. I'm still thinking about some of the things you told me last night."

I creep back towards the bedroom, still within earshot, but out of sight.

"He'll be okay," says Mark. "He loves it here and he likes working at Cherry Smash with Ian and Danny. It's all cool."

"I hope so. I don't mean to sound like my mother, but you've been through rehab a few times. You're strong. Drew's already relapsed from what you've told me, and he tried to kill himself."

"I'll make sure he's okay. I promise."

"So, what are you two doing for Thanksgiving?"

"Hell, if I know," says Mark.

"Then I'll have you guys over at my place."

Kristi mentions that one of her girlfriends will be there, too. I don't catch her name. I edge closer to the kitchen, so I can hear better.

"Is she good looking?" asks Mark.

"Already bored with me?" laughs Kristi.

"No. I was thinking about Drew."

"Drew would probably love her. She's beautiful and bright and has great taste in music, but she was in rehab not so long ago. She's living with her mom in Beverly Hills right now."

"Sounds like she'd be perfect for Drew. They have rehab in common."

"That's what I'm worried about."

When there's a pause in the conversation I make my way to the kitchen. They see me and say 'good morning' in unison.

"Morning," I say. "Man, I slept like a rock."

"Did you go to that party with Danny last night?" asks Mark.

"No, I bailed. I was way too tired. The tour caught up with me."

"I'll make a fresh pot of coffee," says Kristi.

"Thanks, Kristi."

When she returns, Kristi asks, "So, what do you two do for food around here? The refrigerator is empty."

"I've taken Drew to Nova Express for pizza and Pink's."

"Mark, that's garbage food. You need to take care of yourself. When was your last check up?"

"I don't know. I'm okay. Drew's the one with a heart murmur."

"Gee, thanks," I say. "Way to throw me under the bus."

"Well, you both need to take care of yourselves. I swear, you two are like fucking infants."

Mark and I laugh.

"I'm going to take you two somewhere healthy for lunch."

"I need to work in the studio this afternoon," says Mark. "I'm on a roll with some of the new songs."

"I'll take Drew, then, and bring something back for you."

Kristi takes me to a health food joint on Fairfax, the kind of place Granola probably frequents when he's not on tour. I gaze at the menu.

"It's not that bad, I promise," says Kristi. "The veggie burgers are great."

"Sounds good. I need to be better about health and exercise. I walked a lot when I lived in Boston. Mark likes to walk, too. He almost never drives, even though he has a sweet ride."

"I'm not a fanatic but I go to the gym twice a week and I like to hike in Runyon Canyon. The full trail is three miles long and you get some spectacular views of downtown L.A. I try to go there every weekend."

"I could get into that," I say. "I used to be a competitive runner."

"Ha! An ex-jock turned rocker, like Mark. No wonder you two are so close. It's like you're his kid brother."

I don't quite know how to word it, so I just blurt out, "So, are you and Mark an item again? That's so amazing after all these years."

"It is," she says. "We're trying not to rush things. Time is on our side, for once. In high school, everything felt so hectic, especially after my parents sent me away, but you know that."

"Yeah, that sucks. So, your parents hated Mark that much?"

"In retrospect, maybe not as much as I thought. I was rebellious, and they thought Mark was a bad influence because he was such an under-achiever. He didn't care about anything except me and music back then. Did he tell you about the time we ran away to New York to see The Dead Boys?"

"No."

"That would have been a great addition to your article. Anyway, it happened during spring break. I was on the phone with a friend from New York and she said that she was seeing The Dead Boys the next evening. A light bulb flashed in my head; they were Mark's favorite band. We saw them with Devo at the Agora, just after Christmas, and Mark couldn't stop talking about it. When I told him about the New York show, he was like, let's go! I lied to my parents and said I was sleeping over at a friend's house and Mark told his mom that he was going to hang out with Coop for a few days. He had the run of the house. Mark's mom never paid attention to what he did."

"So, you guys drove to New York?"

"We took a Greyhound. We didn't want to risk getting a car stolen. We got a room at the Chelsea Hotel. Mark had a fake ID, but no one cared in those days. New York in the seventies was a war zone, at least that part of the city. Mark had never been there and was mesmerized by all the places he had only read about in magazines. It was such a crazy night. We saw The Dead Boys and after the gig, Mark told Stiv he was from Cleveland. The guys took an immediate liking to him and we partied with them until like four in the morning. I was so fucking hungover on the bus the next day. We got busted when we returned. Mark's mom ran into Coop's mom at the supermarket and she called my parents. Mark and I talked about our New York adventure last night. He said that Stiv remembered him when he started working for The Lords of the New Church."

"Wow. That's a great story. Your reunion with Mark is almost too good to be true."

"All the best stories are."

My White Devil

It takes Mark a few days before he asks if I have any Thanksgiving plans.

"None that I know of. Catalina Coast are playing at Three Clubs. They're open on Thanksgiving. I'll probably catch that."

Mark tells me what I already overheard about Kristi's mysterious house guest and says, "I think the plan is that we're going to Three Clubs after dinner. I've been promising Skip and Tommy that I'd see them play for ages."

"Cool. So, what's Kristi's friend's name? What's her story?"

"Shit, I forgot her name. I don't know, just what I told you. She's an artistic rich chick, trying to kick a coke habit."

I accomplish a few things over the shortened holiday work week, including a long chat with Eddie Zane. Eddie and Ian have ironed out a ten-song album, clocking in at around thirty-three minutes. Danny expresses concern about the length, noting that albums tend to be longer these days, now that CDs have become the preferred format.

"Fuck that shit," Ian says. "None of The Stooges albums were much more than half an hour. We need to leave people wanting more and I want to press it on vinyl, too. Anything longer and it will sound like shit on a turntable."

We agree on two tracks for a limited edition seven-inch, about half of which will be sent to magazines and college radio stations to try and generate a buzz for the album. During my chat with Eddie, I extract some choice pull quotes for the bio. It's fun work and I no longer feel stressed and anxious, like I did in Boston.

The only reminder from my past life is an email from Emily, wondering where I am. I bite the bullet and phone her, telling her that I gave up the Boston apartment, that I started a new job in L.A.

"So, were you ever going to tell me?"

"Eventually. I'm not very good at this kind of stuff."

"No, but you're great at disappearing. You would have been a great magician."

"That's not fair. We barely see each other anymore, so what difference does it make if I live in Boston or L.A.?"

There's a long pause before she says, "I guess there isn't, but the distance makes me sad, that's all."

"For a long time, you were all I ever wanted, but I have to move on."

She starts crying and says, "Don't hurt yourself. And stay in touch."

"I will," I say, before joking, "besides, I need to be on your good side. I'm counting on you for some good reviews."

She laughs, and we're sort of back to normal. I tell her about Death Trip and my little circle of friends: Mark, Danny, and Ian. I don't mention Kristi out of fear that a happy love story might make her sad. She doesn't mention Benjamin.

Mark and I drive to Kristi's on Thanksgiving. She tells us not to bring anything, that she stocked up at Bristol Farms, which Mark tells me is an upscale supermarket chain.

"She must have expensive tastes," I joke. "She wouldn't let me pay for lunch the other day, and that wasn't cheap."

"Her dad died a few years ago. She inherited a lot. Trust me, she's not living on a teacher's salary."

"Sorry about her dad."

"I am, too, even though he never liked me. Maybe he would now. Who knows?"

Kristi lives in a large old apartment building. Mark tells me that it was once a hotel. It's next door to a sleazy motel called the French Cottage.

"Ah, the French Cottage," says Mark. "Someone could write a book about the shit that's gone down there, but dead men tell no tales. It's been a rock 'n' roll drug haven forever. I think Hendrix may have even crashed there for a time. There was this chick named Monica I used to hook up with, a trust fund kid from Louisville or Lexington. Her family breeds racehorses. She was just nineteen. She was a total rock 'n' roll chick, mainly metal, but she liked the darker side of punk, too, like The Damned, Lords of the New Church, and Solarstar. We'd do blow and have sex at sleazy motels, living out her groupie fantasies. I used to call her my White Devil. You know that Bunnymen song, right? Ian Mac supposedly wrote it about his cocaine ills. Anyway, Monica and I didn't last long. I got sober, met you, and got my life together. I'm guessing she's either dead, at home on the farm, or still chasing the dream."

Kristi buzzes us in and we take a miniature Soviet-sized elevator to the third floor. Someone has scrawled 'Informer, a licky boom boom down' in sharpie inside the elevator.

"Fucking Snow graffiti," I say. "That's got to be a first."

Mark laughs and starts singing the chorus to the forgotten Canadian rapper's biggest hit.

Kristi greets us at the door and leads us to the living room. The girl sitting on the couch is the blonde who bummed a smoke off me at Three Clubs.

"Hey, Mark and Drew, this is Vanessa."

"Nice to meet you," says Mark, reaching out his hand.

"Nice to meet you," I say.

She smiles and says, "You don't remember me, do you, Drew?"

"Uh, yeah," I say, a little confused. "We met last week at Three Clubs."

She gives me a knowing wink and says, "No, silly, you need to go back a lot further than that."

"Wait, Vanessa from Rome?"

"You two know each other?" says Kristi.

I tell them the story of how I traveled to Italy during spring break in 1986, when I was studying in England. While in Rome I met Vanessa at a coffee shop. She was traveling with her mom, the world-famous romance novelist Suzanne Dane. One of Dane's novels had been optioned for a movie, which was being filmed in Rome, and Dane was there as a consultant. When I learned that Vanessa was just sixteen to my twenty-one, my mood quickly turned platonic, but we spent a fantastic day together, visiting tourist sites and a cool record store called Transmission, before having an expensive dinner on her mom's tab at the Excelsior.

"I knew you looked familiar," I tell Vanessa, "but I couldn't place it. It was bugging me all week."

"I thought you looked familiar, too, but I didn't make the connection until Kristi mentioned your name, and then it all made sense. Drew from Rome! You never did write to me."

"I know that feeling," says Kristi.

Mark looks uncomfortable, until Kristi gives him a playful jab in the chest. "I'm just teasing you, honey. Help me in the kitchen and let these kids catch up."

I sit next to Vanessa. The last time I saw her she was just a kid. I don't know what to say.

"Don't be so nervous," she says. "I won't bite. So, what have you been doing with yourself all these years?"

"I was in Dublin and Boston before coming here."

"How did you end up in Ireland?"

"I was married to an Irish girl. It didn't work out."

"Sorry," she says.

"We split up five years ago. Ancient history."

I'm hoping Vanessa doesn't think I'm full of excess baggage.

"What about you?" I ask.

"I'm still an artist. I have a solo show next spring in Hollywood. I went to CalArts and got a BFA. Then I took a few years off to work at a gallery on Melrose, before returning to CalArts for an MFA. In retrospect, too much school, but that's how I met Kristi. I wasn't a writing major, but she was a great teacher. I had a lot of fun taking Kristi's and Nicole Panter's classes. Nicole used to manage The Germs and write for *Pee-wee's Playhouse*."

"She must have had some cool stories about Darby Crash."

"Not really. Nicole said that managing The Germs was like babysitting a bunch of five-year-old boys. Kristi told me that you work for a record label."

"I do. Hopefully, Death Trip won't be as hard to work with as The Germs."

"Who are Death Trip?"

"They're this band we just signed from Detroit. They're like a cross between The Stooges and The Jesus and Mary Chain."

"Sounds up my alley. I'm still stuck in the eighties. I got into The Chemical Brothers and Crystal Method for a hot second, but I tend to always return to my favorite high school records."

"Do you still paint to The Church?" I ask.

"You remembered that! I do, but I've moved on from *Heyday* to *Priest = Aura*. That's as far into the nineties as I go."

"I'm with you on the nineties with a few exceptions. There are some great Irish bands that got lost in the Britpop shuffle, like Into Paradise and Whipping Boy."

"I've never heard of them. You'll have to play them for me sometime."

"Sure. I'd love to hang out again," I say.

Kristi interrupts us and says, "Dinner's almost ready. Are you guys okay with Ginger Ale?"

"Sure," we say in tandem.

Kristi leaves.

"Not a drinker?" asks Vanessa.

"No. I'm sober."

"Is that how you know Mark?"

"Yeah. I interviewed Mark for a magazine article back in '87, but we became friends doing hard time in San Clemente."

"You're not alone," she says. "I spent a few months at Promises in Malibu."

I pretend that it's news to me and joke, "I guess we have rehab and great taste in music in common."

"It's tough staying clean," she says. "I especially miss wine."

"I hear you. I cheat with weed, but that's never triggered me. It also helps that I left Boston. I feel like I can reinvent myself here."

"Sometimes, I wish I could leave L.A. Most of my old friends are still cokeheads."

I take her hand and say, "Here's to new friendships, then."

She squeezes my hand and says, "To new friendships."

After dinner, Mark and I share a joint in the kitchen while we wash the dishes.

"Hey, what's going on in there?" says Kristi when she hears Mark, singing the chorus to *Informer*.

"I thought I was the only one who noticed that graffiti," blurts Vanessa.

"I suppose we should start getting ready for Three Clubs," says Kristi.

"Sure," says Mark. "I haven't seen the Urinator and Granola since the tour ended."

"Who are they?" asks Vanessa.

"Skip and Tommy from Catalina Coast," says Kristi. "They all had silly names for each other on the tour."

"Skip was the Urinator because he peed a lot and Tommy was Granola because of his vegan diet," I say.

"What did they call you, Drew?" asks Vanessa.

"Drew was the Dark Horse," says Mark "because he was always full of surprises. He's a deep and moody guy."

"That's how I like them," Vanessa says. She takes my hand. I'm excited, but also scared that I'm falling for her so fast.

We take Vanessa's car to Three Clubs. She has a '64 Ford Falcon Futura in a shade Mark immediately identifies as dynasty green. Vanessa is impressed, and Mark tells her about his Caddy.

"Man, what's up with all the cool cars here?" I ask. "Everyone I've met has one."

"Not me," says Kristi. "I drive a fucking Accord."

"It's the weather," says Mark. "If I lived somewhere bleak like Cleveland or Detroit, I'd drive a piece of shit."

Vanessa takes my hand when we enter Three Clubs. The four of us run into Danny Scorpio at the bar. He's nursing a bourbon and coke. When Kristi and Vanessa excuse themselves to go to the ladies' room, Danny says, "Is that the chick you were talking to last week?"

"Yeah."

"Turns out that she's friends with Kristi and that we actually met thirteen years ago."

"Man, that's a trip."

"Tell me about it," says Mark. "I keep feeling like I'm in a dream or I'm dead or something and that I finally found Kristi again in the afterlife."

"Dude, you're getting too cosmic for me," says Danny. "So, Drew, off topic, but I think I swung a deal with Catalina Coast."

"No shit?"

"Just a seven-inch. Their singer Grant wants to hold out for a major label deal for the album, but I told Skip and Tommy about the Death Trip single and they're all on board."

"Right on," I say. I find myself saying 'right on' and 'yeah, dude' a lot in L.A. It's that kind of place. The mellow pace of life is suiting me.

"Ian's stoked," says Danny. "We'll talk more later, but he wants to branch out and create an offshoot label called Cherry Smash 2000, exclusively for Death Trip, Catalina Coast, and anyone else we might sign."

"Here's to Cherry Smash 2000, then. What's Ian up to tonight?"

"He's getting sloshed at Cat & Fiddle."

Mark chuckles. "Same old Ian. It's been his home away from home forever."

We rejoin the girls in the main room, where Catalina Coast are setting up. Skip and Tommy look like two completely different people now that they're back in their regular band, having traded in the Chelsea boots and skinny black jeans they wore on the Solarstar tour for boot-cut 517s, Clarks, and western pearl-button shirts. The singer Grant is strikingly handsome, like a male model. He reminds me of James Taylor in *Two-Lane Black Top* with his long brown hair, denim-on-denim ensemble, and a silk scarf.

While they're part of the same scene, Catalina Coast are more commercial than Beachwood Sparks; more pop, less psychedelic. During one song, Grant even throws in a few lines from a Monkees song. The kids dig them, especially the girls, who crowd near the front.

One of them, a short brunette, looks out of place in skintight leather pants.

Mark grabs my arm and leads me to the back of the room.

"Fuck," he says. "That chick in the leather…"

"Uh, yeah."

"That's the crazy bitch, Monica. You know, the chick I was telling you about."

"No need to fret, man. It looks like she's preoccupied."

"I guess you're right. It's just a reminder of why I don't like to go out. You don't know anyone here, but my demons are everywhere."

I bump into Anton and he asks if I'm enjoying the show.

"It's okay," I say.

"More like the last train to dullsville," he quips as he walks away.

When the band finishes, Mark and I go outside and pass around a funny cigarette. A few minutes later, Vanessa and Kristi join us.

"So, what did you think?" asks Kristi.

"It was okay," I say. "They're a great-looking band, but it felt manufactured. I liked Beachwood Sparks more, but I suppose I need to be enthusiastic now that we're putting out a Catalina Coast single."

I hear a voice from behind. We turn around. It's Monica. She moves in on Mark, a little too close for comfort, placing her hand on his shoulder.

"Hey stranger, how's it going? The Solarstar show last week was so awesome." The words ooze out of her like she's a porn actress.

"Thanks," says Mark. "The tour was fun. I've just been taking it easy."

He introduces Kristi as his girlfriend, which doesn't faze Monica in the slightest.

"Nice to meet you," she says before refocusing on Mark. "So, I haven't seen you in years. Where have you been?"

"Rehab," Mark deadpans.

"So, you haven't seen Elliott in a while, then?" she asks, not quite picking up on Mark's sarcasm.

"No reason to, but I enjoy his music and wish him well."

"Next time I'm at the Roost, I'll tell him that. He was asking about you last week."

Monica leaves and I can't help but look at her ass for longer than I should.

"Earth to Drew," laughs Vanessa.

"Sorry," I say.

"Nothing to be sorry about. I was checking out that ass out, too. She's kind of hot, but in a hot mess kind of way. If she hung around us any longer, I would have done a line off her pores. The cocaine was practically dripping out of her."

Hollywood Nights

When we leave the club, Vanessa whispers something to Kristi and they both laugh.

"What do you think they're talking about?" I ask Mark.

"Chick stuff."

We return to Kristi's place, Vanessa says to me, "I'm going to borrow you for a while, if that's okay. The night is young."

"Be careful, kids," teases Kristi.

Mark gives me a knowing smile. I roll with it, thinking how weird it is that for the second time in a month a girl has asked to 'borrow' me. Whatever was affecting my game in Boston has washed away on my cross-country journey. Vanessa and I head east on Hollywood Boulevard, driving past a series of shops. Vanessa says that they tend to be novelty stores, hawking tacky Hollywood souvenirs or rock 'n' roll and sex-themed establishments, selling overly-priced band T-shirts and bondage gear.

"Have you ever been to Jumbo's Clown Room?" asks Vanessa.

"Uh, no."

"It's a strip club, but not a cheesy one like Cheetahs or Crazy Girls. Courtney Love used to dance there. It's more like a dive bar. The girls are topless, but not fully nude."

"Cool," I say, trying to figure out where this evening is headed. The chemistry feels right, and I can sense that Vanessa finds me attractive, but we're both vulnerable. I feel like I'm starting from the wrong place, like I did with Emily. Maybe there's never a right place? I try to think of times in my life when everything felt right, and I can't. I'm scared that we're moving too fast. I figured that L.A. would be a good place to recoup and get over Emily, maybe have a few casual encounters, like I did with Rose in Nashville. The three main women in my life – my first girlfriend Christine, Claire, and Emily – all ended up leaving me. I'm afraid to make that kind of commitment again.

I'm awkward in strip clubs, a feeling akin to having your parents discover your porn stash when you're a kid. Vanessa is right, though. Jumbo's is a dive, about the size of a small living room with a jukebox in the corner. Half of the punters aren't even paying attention to the dancers. It's more of a rock 'n' roll crowd than a rowdy bachelor party atmosphere. The strippers are down to earth, too; more tattooed than your typical dancer with less silicon to boot.

Vanessa orders a couple of Sprites.

"I don't think I'll ever get used to drinking soda in a bar," she says.

"I hear you. It was rough being around so much booze on the Solarstar tour. At least I had Mark to keep me company."

"And you have me now."

I take her hand.

"From what Kristi has told me, Mark had a real rough time."

"Yeah. The nineties are a blur for him. He's been in rehab three times."

"Once was enough for me."

"Ditto," I say. "I've only done coke a few times, but never enough to get hooked like Mark."

"I occasionally miss it," she says. "I started doing it more for work than pleasure because I liked it better than coffee. Like I always say, coffee is a shitty substitute for cocaine. I'd get these incredible rushes when I was painting, but it turned me into an asshole."

"I guess I didn't miss out then."

"You seem more like the dark, romantic drinker type, like a film noir detective," she says.

"I suppose so, but after a while, drinking made me severely depressed. I'm afraid my Bukowski phase is a fading memory."

"So, did you have a trigger moment, like when you knew you needed help?"

I tell her about my half-assed suicide attempt.

"I forced other people to make the decision for me. I feel shitty about that."

"Being unhappy isn't a crime. I hope you're happy now."

"I am."

"Well, that's good."

"So, what about you?" I ask. "How did you end up in rehab?"

"I was scared straight. I was dating a dealer. I thought he was small-time at first. He would give me free stuff – not that I couldn't afford it – but he was trying to impress me. I was out with him one night and he said that he needed to stop at his second apartment and I was like, you have two apartments? It turned out that he rented this little hole-in-the-wall to conduct business. There were scales all over the place and a lot of guns. There was an MK16 leaning against one of the walls."

"Wow."

"Yeah, crazy as hell. I called my mom the next day and told her everything. I'm an only child, and we're close. I was only five when my dad died. She was barely thirty. He had a heart attack out of the blue."

"Fuck. Mark lost his dad when he was young. That's so sad."

"I know. Kristi told me, but my mom kept her shit together, unlike Mark's."

"I gathered as much when you told me about her in Rome."

"And she's sold a million more since. She's a machine. She's slowed down, but she was way focused on her work when I was a kid. It was her way to get over my dad."

"How did they meet? I remember you told me he was a producer."

"You have a good memory, Drew. You wasted a lot of years not getting to know me."

"Sorry."

"I'm teasing you. You wouldn't have wanted me when I was in my early twenties. I turn thirty in March. Crazy. Anyway, one of my mom's early novels got turned into a movie and my dad was the producer. It was love at first sight. I hope I'm not fucking up by saying this, Drew, but I feel like that with you right now."

I go silent and she says, "Sorry, I'm fucking things up, aren't I?"

"No, I feel the same," I say. "I was thinking about you all week before I knew who you were. It feels weird that this is happening now with everything that's going on with Mark and Kristi. I guess they're responsible for us being here right now."

"Actually, you are. Your article was the catalyst. I do have a confession to make," says Vanessa.

I panic for a second, thinking that maybe she's going to tell me that she's married or something, but there's no ring on her finger.

"Nothing sinister," she says. "Don't look so worried. It's just that I've kept tabs on you. I remembered that you wanted to be a writer when we first met and when I got my first computer and email account, I started looking for you online. I found a few of your old stories from *AP* and *Spin*."

"I'm glad someone read them. It's not an easy way to make a living, nor is working for a label. Ian's not exactly paying me a mint and, sooner or later, I'll need to get my own place. Mark doesn't seem to mind me crashing with him, but this stuff with Kristi is so sudden. Who knows where that's headed?"

"Kristi has her shit together. I can attest to that. She's my best friend. I stay with her a few nights a week."

"Is it tough living at home?"

"Not at all. My mom's house is huge and there's a small guest house, where I stay. My mom jokes that it's my halfway house, but it's like living at a resort. She has a pool. Want to go swimming?"

"Like right now?"

"Yeah. My mom's in Palm Springs for the weekend. Not that she would mind. She'd like you."

"It's sixty degrees outside. We'll freeze our asses off."

"The pool is permanently set at ninety-five degrees. My mom's a freeze baby."

"Sure, but I don't have a swim suit."

"That's the point."

We watch a dancer, who manages to gyrate while juggling two firesticks. Vanessa hands me a few singles and asks me to slip them into the dancer's G-string on our way out the door.

As we drive down Sunset towards Beverly Hills, I can't help but think of that awful Bob Seger song that was a hit when I was a kid. The cliched lyrics about the midwestern boy, hanging out with a rich girl. Yet, here I am, a Michigan boy, in a similar situation, on my way to a mansion in Beverly Hills to presumably make love to a girl, way out of my league.

When we get to her mom's place, Vanessa punches in a code to open an impressive gate worthy of Fort

Knox. We park in front of the main house and walk hand-in-hand on a path that takes us to a secluded palm tree-laden area where the pool and guest house are located. The guest house is larger than Mark's real home.

"Man, I could get used to living here," I say when we enter.

The guest house is tastefully decorated, the furniture in perfect symmetry, other than an easel in the living room, placed next to a small table cluttered with paints and brushes.

"I know, I'm spoiling the aesthetic," says Vanessa, reading my mind, "but it's a great place to work."

"The studio adds to the decor," I say. "I'm afraid to touch anything."

"Don't be," says Vanessa. "My mom's not a tyrant."

"Cool," I say as I take a seat on a plush velvet couch. Vanessa joins me.

"I could get used to this," I say.

"I'm not in a hurry to leave," she admits, "but I know I need to. I don't want to get a rep as one of these spoiled rich bitch types, like Paris Hilton."

"Well, I've never seen you in the tabloid press, so that's a start."

"It's because of my mom. Not that many people know who I am. She never let the press take pictures of me when I was a kid, even the big magazines, like *Vanity Fair*. She thinks celebrities who show off their kids are tacky."

"The whole *Less Than Zero* existence; famous for being rich and stupid."

"Exactly. I grew up with those kinds of people but, thankfully, I'm good at avoiding them. I was the weird art school punk at Beverly Hills High. I graduated right before *90210* came out, thank god."

"So, what do you see in me? I don't have much to offer, except a good record collection."

"Sold," she says. "I like you because you did everything you said you would. You became a writer. I don't need to be around rich guys. I have all the money I need, and you don't seem to give a fuck about it, so I know you don't like me for that reason."

She edges closer to me.

"Don't be so nervous," she says. "I'm not sixteen anymore."

She kisses me, and I return the favor.

"Let's go to the bedroom," she says.

"I'm not too skinny, am I?" she asks as she undresses in front of me. "I lost a lot of weight when I was sick, but it's coming back."

"No, you're hot. You're perfect."

We make love. Once I get past the fact that she's not a kid anymore, it's fast, passionate, and effortless, like we've been lovers for years. Afterwards, we take a dip in the pool. It's sunrise when we go to bed. When we wake up in the early afternoon, Vanessa calls Kristi to let her know we're okay. We make plans to meet them on Sunday for a hike in Runyon Canyon.

Vanessa kisses me before leading me to the shower for a quickie. Two months ago, I was a depressed, emotional wreck and now, dare I say it, I'm happy.

Watching the Detectives

When we get dressed, we decide to go out for lunch. It feels weird being without Mark. I wonder if he feels the same; the dynamic of our friendship having changed so abruptly. A week ago, we were like a rock 'n' roll version of *The Odd Couple* – though in our case, we both fall into the Felix Unger neat freak category – and now we've nosedived into serious relationships. Kristi appeared into Mark's life out of thin air – well, mainly due to the interview I conducted on the fly (talk about fate) – and just as I was beginning to feel like a third wheel with Kristi spending so much time at our place, Vanessa turns up. It's like she's claimed me. I'm excited and can't stop thinking about her, but I'm nervous and scared that it's going to crash and burn.

The traffic is heavy as we drive down Beverly Boulevard.

"What's going on?" I ask.

"Oh shit, I forgot it's Black Friday. Hollywood and Beverly Hills are going to be crazy."

"Christ, it's that time of the year already? California has fucked up my body clock. It still feels like summer to me."

"The endless summer, as the surfers used to say. Have you seen that documentary?"

"No," I say.

"You should. I'm not into surfing but there's some cool footage, especially of Hawaii in the fifties and sixties before things got all commercial and the real estate market blew up."

"I've never been to Hawaii."

"I haven't either. I'm not exactly the water sports type."

"That's a relief," I say. "I was hoping you wouldn't ask me to pee on you."

"You have a dirty mind, Drew. I like it. I think we'll get along. So, where should we eat? I'm starved."

"You tell me. Anywhere but Hollywood I guess."

"How about the Saugus Café?" suggests Vanessa. "It's not that far of a drive."

"Where's that?"

"In Newhall, near CalArts," says Vanessa. "It's a great diner. It's where James Dean had his last meal before he died."

"Death and rock 'n' roll. I'm game."

We head north out of Hollywood into the Santa Clarita Valley, merging onto the 5 Freeway, which extends along the entire west coast from Mexico to Canada.

"Gene Vincent is buried in Newhall, too," Vanessa says, as she maneuvers the Futura through traffic.

"You're like a walking pop culture encyclopedia," I say.

"I was a film major before I switched to fine arts," says Vanessa. "I love Hollywood history. All the old movies, especially the pre-code era."

The diner is shaped like a railroad car with booths alongside the windows facing out onto the street and a long counter with stools, opposite the kitchen, daily specials written on several chalkboards. Framed photos of celebrities who frequented the joint, including James Dean, John Wayne, and Marlene Deitrich line the walls.

"What's good here?" I ask.

"The all-day breakfast menu is always great," says Vanessa. "So are the chicken fried steaks."

We opt for the steaks, which we wolf down with multiple cups of coffee.

"So, what else is out here?" I ask.

"I can show you my old place on Race Street."

"Race Street, as in race riots?"

"No, as in drag races," says Vanessa. "It got its name from all the illegal racing that used to go on there."

Race Street is in the barrio. As we drive through the neighborhood, I can't help but notice all the unsupervised kids running around amongst the stray dogs and chickens.

"My mom thought I was crazy for wanting to live here, but it's safe; everyone looks after each other. The only downside was being woken up early on weekend mornings. There's always a Quinceanera going on."

"What's that?" I ask.

"It's this big celebration Mexicans have when their daughters turn fifteen; it marks their passage into womanhood. They book DJs and bands, the full works. I can't imagine how much debt some of these families rack up."

Afterwards, we drive to the Vasquez Rocks, a natural park with breathtaking formations that are millions of years old. Vanessa points out a sequence that I remember from an episode of *Star Trek*.

"It's called Kirk's Rock," she says. "It was also in *Bill and Ted's Bogus Journey*!"

Vanessa regales me with more tales of old Hollywood, of places that I must see.

"I can't get enough of it," she says. "I have a huge book collection. It's all packed up at my mom's house for now. I can't wait until we get a place... I mean, I get a place. Sorry, I keep pushing you too fast."

"It can be us," I say.

She smiles and says, "I can't wait."

It hasn't even been twenty-four hours, but at this moment I feel content to spend the rest of my life with Vanessa, but I keep the thought to myself. When we get home, Vanessa and I go for a swim before taking a nap. It's dark when we wake up.

"Feel like watching a movie?" she says. "There's always something decent on Turner Classic."

"Sounds good to me."

There's a Bogart double feature; *Casablanca* and *The Maltese Falcon*.

"Luck of the draw," I say. "I love both of those films."

"I do, too," says Vanessa, "but with reservations."

"What don't you like?"

"The endings. Ingrid Berman picks the wrong guy in *Casablanca*."

"Laszlo too much of a do-gooder for you?"

"Something like that. I tend to fall for moody, depressed guys."

"You've won the lottery with me, though I am trying to work on being mildly depressed. I take my meds every day."

"I can live with that."

"What about *The Maltese Falcon*?" I ask. "I don't like the ending either. Kind of a dick move on Bogart's part. You sleep with your asshole partner's wife and then you develop some bullshit code of honor after he gets killed?"

"Exactly, right? Brigid O'Shaughnessy may have been a hot mess, but I would have let her get away with murder."

*

I'm alone when I wake up the next morning. I throw on a pair of jeans and find Vanessa at work in her makeshift studio.

"Morning," she says as she kisses me on the cheek. "Brush your teeth and I'll give you a proper wake up kiss."

"Will do," I say, "but I could use some coffee first."

"There's a fresh pot in the kitchen. I couldn't sleep, so I thought I'd get some work done."

"Is this for the show you're doing in the spring?"

"Yeah, I have most of it done, but I want to do at least two more paintings."

The Church's *Hindsight* CD is playing in the background.

"Good choice," I say. "I miss my record collection."

"You didn't do anything stupid and sell it before you moved here, did you?"

"No! My brother Paul has a box of vinyl and my CDs stored at his place in Cambridge, along with my stereo. I downsized my collection a bit before I moved, but I've kept all the favorites. Thankfully, Mark has a great collection to keep me at bay."

"My records and stereo are in my bedroom in the main house, but I tend to listen to the same six CDs over and over while I paint. I could use some new inspiration. Feel like going to Aron's? You were telling me about some good Irish bands you liked."

"Sure," I say. "Most of the Whipping Boy and Into Paradise stuff is hard to find because they were released on small indie labels, but they were both briefly on major labels. We might get lucky."

"This will be so fun," she says with a huge smile on her face. "Remember that store in Rome we went to?"

"Yeah, Transmission! I still have the vinyl copy of *Psychocandy* you bought me there."

We manage to track down used copies of Whipping Boy's *Heartworm* and Into Paradise's *Churchtown* for $4.99 each. I feel saddened that two of my all-time favorite albums have been relegated to bargain bin status.

Vanessa pops *Churchtown* into her car's CD player, the only modern upgrade to her beloved Futura. She asks if there's anything else I want to do.

"Can we visit the tar pits?"

"Sure," she says.

It feels weird to listen to a gloomy, albeit mesmerizing album on a beautiful sunny day, but Vanessa digs it.

"I can definitely paint to this," she says. "I love the singer's voice; it's so intense."

"They were a great band. I was lucky enough to see them a few times when I lived in Dublin."

"Do you miss Ireland?"

"I do at times, but I have so many bad memories. I'm not sure if I'm ready to visit there again. Maybe someday."

"You need to create new memories. We should visit Ireland together. My mom's side of the family is Irish; it would be cool to learn more about my roots."

I pause.

"Shit, I'm moving too fast on you again, aren't I?"

"No. I'm just nervous. I keep fucking up relationships. I don't want to hurt you."

"You won't. We're right for each other."

"So, you're psychic?"

"Hardly," she laughs, "but we work well together. We're creative, but our passions are different enough that we complement each other. I want to have what my mom experienced with my dad, even if it turns out to be brief. She's never found anyone to replace him. It makes me so sad."

We talk more as we walk around the tar pits. The park outside is a bit cheesy, but I feel like a kid again, marveling at the large-scale models of mammoths and sabre tooth tigers.

"The museum inside is better," says Vanessa. "There's this huge display of Dire Wolf and Sabre Tooth Tiger skulls."

"So," I say as we gaze at the skulls and bones inside. "I meant to ask what brought you to Three Clubs the other week. Are you a regular there? It seems like a fun scene. I haven't been this excited about new music in a good decade. There are so many great bands in Los Angeles."

"I've been there a few times. I do like it. One of my girlfriends has a huge crush on Corey from The Warlocks. She's too shy to say anything to him, though. It's silly. We keep going there and she keeps freezing up. If I want something or someone, I never keep it secret."

Pop Faggotry

On my first day at Cherry Smash, Danny warned me about Ian's 'immediate action' moods. I experience one on Monday morning. The day starts nice and mellow with Danny and me drinking coffee at our desks, catching up on emails, and talking about our weekends. I tell him about my adventures with Vanessa, including our excursion in Runyon Canyon. I fared better than expected, but we had to take a few breaks to allow Mark to catch his breath. "Fuck, I'm out of shape," he kept telling us. Danny tells me about a night out at the Roost, where he ended up having a long conversation with Elliott Smith and Anton.

"They were both lit, but it was fascinating to pick their brains. I felt like I was in the presence of greatness. I can't wait to hear their new records, but, man, I wish they would take better care of themselves. We don't need a Hendrix or Morrison-like casualty in our scene."

He starts to tell me about a girl he picked up when Ian barges in with a mail tub, overflowing with padded envelopes.

"Okay, lads, time to get to work," says Ian.

"Immediate action," Danny whispers.

"What's that?" says Ian.

"The Action," says Danny. "I was telling Drew about a bootleg I had of their post-mod stuff, when they got into a nice California groove."

I can barely contain myself.

"Ah, great band," says Ian, "and that's what I hope we'll find in this bucket full of shite. We're off to a nice start with Cherry Smash 2000, but let's see if we can find a gem or two in here. This is a year's worth of demos that I haven't bothered to listen to. You know the drill, Danny. If the bio sounds interesting, we'll give it a listen on the boombox. If they namecheck influences we hate, we chuck the CD into the trash. Follow my lead."

Ian opens an envelope and removes a CD and bio. He scans over it and says, "They claim to be influenced by The Dandy Warhols but look at the photo. One of the guys is wearing a football jersey and his name is TD. What kind of bollocks is that?"

"Maybe he's an ex-jock," laughs Danny. "TD is probably short for Touchdown."

"More like Total Douche," says Ian, "and they look fat; too much pie, too few drugs."

Ian tosses the CD into the trash.

"Okay, you're next Drew."

I laugh as I reach into the tub. My package includes a photo of four guys in matching suits and mod haircuts.

"They look sharp," I say.

"Promising," says Ian as he glances at the photo. "What's in the bio?"

"Says they're influenced by classic mod icons, like The Who and The Jam, and power pop legends Cheap Trick..."

"Throw it out," says Ian.

"What for?" says Danny. "I thought you liked The Who and The Jam. You're the most mod dude on the planet. What the fuck has gotten into you?"

"It's not The Who or The Jam I'm complaining about, it's fucking Cheap Trick. I hate Cheap Trick. They're my least favorite band, ever."

Ian pronounces Cheap Trick the British way, with an extended pause between the two words.

"Oh, come on, man," says Danny. "You don't like Cheap Trick? Their early albums are classics." He starts singing *Surrender*.

"Oh, fuck off Danny."

Danny and I laugh before I chime in, telling them how much I loved *Live at Budokan* when I was a kid.

"It's bollocks," says Ian. "Pop faggotry."

"Pop faggotry?" asks Danny. I can almost see his eyes roll.

"Indeed," says Ian. "Power pop is a pussy compromise; bands who are too limp-wristed to be punk, but not brave enough to cross the gay line and become Culture Club. I have more respect for Culture Club and Bronski Beat than I do for fucking Cheap Trick."

Ian grabs the CD from my hand and throws it against the wall, so hard that it shatters, which apparently is a regular occurrence. When he leaves the room, Danny says, "I guess it's my turn now. What are the odds on the next glossy? Railroad tracks or brick wall?"

"I'll go with railroad tracks."

Danny laughs and opens an envelope. It's a goth band from Florida, posing in a graveyard. One of the guys is wearing a white pirate shirt.

"Oh man," I say. "Why the fuck is a goth band sending a CD to a garage rock label?"

"Dude, that happens all the time. No one does their research. Bands blindly send demos to any label they can find an address for."

"And the landfills keep growing."

When Jokers Attack

Eddie Zane is seated on a bench outside baggage claim when I arrive at LAX. I park Vanessa's Futura alongside the curb and get out to greet him. It's a chilly Thursday morning in February – barely sixty degrees – but Eddie's in jeans and a T-shirt, looking quite comfortable. Mark had joked that my blood would thin after a few months in L.A., that I'd start to get cold easily, and he was right. I'm wearing a jean jacket and wish I had taken my leather instead.

Eddie's here for a long weekend. He calls it a recon mission. He wants to check out the scene I keep telling him about in our weekly conversations and he's going to help Mark tweak a few things on the album.

A lot has happened since Thanksgiving. Kristi moved into Mark's place and subleased the McCadden apartment to me and Vanessa. I see Mark when he comes into Cherry Smash for his daily coffee ritual with Ian, but I miss the reduced dude time, much as I love being around Vanessa. Vanessa and I have lunch or dinner with Mark and Kristi several times a week and we've been sticking to our weekend Runyon Canyon hikes. I'm feeling fighting fit for the first time in years.

Danny and I never did find a gem in Ian's mail tub, but the two of us have been making the scene at Three Clubs and other venues, like Spaceland and Silverlake Lounge, keeping our eyes peeled for promising local acts. We especially dig Sunstorm, who have a trippy Verve-meets-early-seventies-Rolling-Stones vibe and The Tyde, who mix sixties and seventies California influences with splashes of UK indie.

Eddie hugs me and says, "Good to see you again, man."

"Likewise."

"Nice wheels," said Eddie as he picks up the CD case of Brian Jonestown Massacre's *Give It Back!* which had been laying on the passenger seat.

"It's my girlfriend Vanessa's car, but she lets me drive it. She's very protective. It's her baby."

"Sounds like a great girl."

"She is. I'm a lucky son of a bitch. You'll get to meet her."

"Cool. I'd date her for the car alone. Good call with BJM. I've been getting into them a lot, lately. Will I get a chance to meet Anton?"

"Most likely. He's not hard to find. He'll probably be at Three Clubs tonight. It's a popular spot on Thursdays. The Tyde are playing. You'll like them."

"Right on."

Anton Newcombe's vocals belt through the car speakers on the infectious flute-driven rave up *Servo*. I lean over to crank up the volume and lose control of the car. I panic and clutch the wheel for dear life as we do a full three-sixty before coming to a complete stop on the side of the road. Fortunately, no one is near us for those precious seconds, which feel like an eternity. I laugh before panting, "Welcome to Los Angeles."

"Rock 'n' Roll," says Eddie, not fazed in the least. "That was fucking rad. I used to do donuts in the snow all the time."

"Same here. Winter ritual for me and my high school buddies."

When we're back on the road, Eddie peppers me with questions about L.A. He's experiencing the same excitement I felt when I first arrived.

"I can't believe I'm here. It's so trippy. I've never seen a palm tree," he says.

I laugh, telling him about my similar reaction.

"Mark's excited about the master," I say, "but he'll want your input. I think he did a great job capturing your live sound."

"Awesome. I can't wait to hear how it all sounds in a proper studio. Turn the amps up to eleven, man!"

Eddie is staying at the Beverly Laurel, a moderately priced hotel, not far from the Cherry Smash offices. After getting Eddie checked in, we walk next door to Swingers. It's a nothing special, above-average diner but Eddie is mesmerized by the menu, as if he's eating at a four-star joint in Paris. "This is so cool," he keeps saying. He's perplexed that there's a grilled cheese sandwich with Avocado.

After lunch, I take Eddie to Cherry Smash. We have a surprise waiting for him, the Death Trip seven-inch, hot off the presses. Eddie is thrilled. The photo on the sleeve is your standard tough guy alleyway pose, copped by numerous bands over the years from the Stones to The Clash to The Dead Boys. However, there's a hint of innocence in the Death Trip snapshot, one of near disbelief, as if the band can't apprehend their good fortune. The A-side is taken from the forthcoming self-titled album, a Stooges/Heartbreakers-influenced heavy-riffing anthem called *Desperate*, while the flip is a cover of *Guitar Army* by cult sixties Detroit garage rockers The Rationals.

Ian gives it a spin it on the office turntable and Eddie bops around the room like a toddler. Mark is with us and Eddie hugs him, repeatedly thanking him for getting the sound right.

"I'll take you to my studio in a bit," says Mark. "We can listen to the album there. Don't be shy. I love it and Drew, Danny and Ian are all on board, but we want you to be happy, too."

"You better be happy," says Ian.

A large group of us have dinner and drinks at the Cat & Fiddle – me, Ian, Mark, Danny, Eddie, plus Vanessa and Kristi – before heading to Three Clubs. At one point, Mark pulls me aside, telling me that Eddie asked him if he knew where he could score some coke.

"So, what did you say?"

"I tried to be polite about it and told him that I'm a recovering addict, and not to mess with that shit. He was like, I only do a bump now and then, but I could see through his bullshit. Hope this doesn't become a problem. If it does, don't say I didn't warn you."

Mark seems less tolerant of Eddie than he was with Tommy and Skip in Nashville. When we get to Three Clubs, Mark parks himself at the bar and catches up with Tami, while Danny and I take Eddie around, introducing him to friends in bands and several writers. Most of the crowd is dressed in denim head to toe. A square looking guy enters the bar with his girlfriend and turns his head in both directions before asking, "Why is everyone dressed like it's the seventies?"

There's a buzz about The Tyde and one can see why when they take the stage. The singer Darren Rademaker has a silky, smooth delivery. Danny is equally enthralled, and we lose track of Eddie, who was already quite intoxicated when we saw him last.

"Think he's okay?" I ask.

"Yeah," says Danny. "He's nice and buzzed. He's probably trying to pick up a chick to take back to the Beverly Laurel."

"He should have brought a few singles as calling cards."

"That might work here. Sometimes, I feel like lying and telling girls I'm in a band. It's an easier way to get laid than saying you work for a record label."

I excuse myself to take a leak. While I'm taking care of business, two guys stumble out of a stall. It's Eddie and a skeezy dude I don't know. Eddie doesn't strike me as a homo, so I'm guessing he got his bump after all.

"Hey Drew," he says as he staggers by.

I nod as I continue to piss. Anton pulls up in the stall next to mine and says, "I hear you guys signed Eddie and the Cruisers."

I laugh and say, "I think you'd like Death Trip."

"I don't mind them," says Anton. "They sent Greg Shaw a demo last year. Eddie bugs me, though. He's a joker."

When The Tyde finish their set, Vanessa and Kristi go outside for a smoke. Mark and Danny head to the stage to say hi to the Rademaker boys, who are packing up their gear. I'm about to join them but decide I could use a few hits from a funny cigarette first. I step outside and spark one up. It feels like meditation – albeit a far less healthy version – as I let Mark's concoction work its magic over a series of long drags.

A female voice asks if I have a light. I turn my head. It's Monica, AKA the White Devil. I've seen her around a few times since Thanksgiving but haven't talked to her. She's wearing tight black jeans and a black tank top underneath a black leather jacket, as if she's copying Kristi's look. Her hair is still jet black, though.

I light her cigarette and she takes a quick drag before saying, "You're Drew, right?"

"Yeah."

"You're friends with Mark, right?"

"Yeah"

"So, how do you guys know each other?"

"Rehab."

"Shame," she says. "I saw you here by your lonesome self and thought you might want to party."

"I might have taken you up on that offer a few years ago, but it's just weed for me these days."

Mark walks past us and joins the girls. He kisses Kristi and Monica squirms. It's clear that she still holds a torch for him.

"So, are Mark and that girl like exclusive?"

"Yeah, they live together. That's pretty exclusive in my book."

"Shame. Mark and I had some good times together. You kind of look alike, like you could be brothers."

I don't say anything. I'm feeling uncomfortable and searching for an exit strategy. Eddie, of all people, rescues me.

"Hey man, how's it hanging, Drew?"

He's obviously done another bump or two since I ran into him in the john. Monica scans him up and down.

"Monica, do you know Eddie? He's visiting from Detroit. We're putting out his album on Cherry Smash in a few months."

She perks up. "What are you called?"

"Death Trip," slurs Eddie.

"As in The Stooges?"

"Yeah, but people keep telling us we sound like Black Rebel Motorcycle Club."

"Not a bad band to be compared to. Do you want to party, Eddie?"

"Always."

Monica winks at me and whispers, "Maybe some other time, Drew."

I shrug it off and say, "Behave yourselves and don't forget, Eddie, I'm supposed to pick you up at noon tomorrow."

"We'll try to behave," says Monica as the two of them walk into the night.

I join Mark and the girls.

Vanessa asks, "So, what was that all about? That skank was all over you."

"She kind of made a pass at me," I admit. "I pawned her off on Eddie."

"She's so gross," says Vanessa.

"She was all over Mark the last time I saw her," says Kristi. "What did she say to you, Drew?"

"She asked me if I wanted to party."

"So, you passed her off on Eddie," says Mark. He's ticked off.

"Dude, if you haven't noticed, Eddie's been doing coke all night. I walked in on him and another guy in the bathroom."

"Whatever," says Mark. "Once the album comes out, I don't give a fuck if that Iggy Pop-wannabee bites the dust. Death sells."

"Let's just go home," says Kristi. "This night has turned into a bummer."

I take Vanessa's hand. She tells me that she doesn't like Eddie. I tell her that Anton called him a joker.

"That makes Monica Harley Quinn."

The Morning After Girl

I drive to the Beverly Laurel, half expecting Eddie to be MIA. Before leaving Three Clubs, Mark and I got into an argument. He told me that I shouldn't have left Eddie alone with Monica. Danny Scorpio took my side.

"It's not like he's Tiny Tim," Danny said. "The dude's been around the block a few times. Hell, I'd fuck Monica if I got the chance, though I'd probably wear at least three condoms for protection."

Kristi and Vanessa laughed while Mark squirmed. It's clear that he hasn't told Kristi about Monica. Probably for the best. Nothing good would come out of that confession.

I knock on Eddie's door and Monica answers. She's wearing black panties and the same tank top she wore last night. It's pushed up a bit, exposing her belly.

"Uh, I'm guessing I came at a bad time," I say. "I can come back later. I'll go to Swingers for coffee or something."

"No, it's okay. Eddie just jumped in the shower. He had a rough night."

"I can imagine," I say. "You seem lively, though."

"I'm a professional partier," she giggles. "I just did a bump. I'm wide awake, but on the down side, it makes me horny as hell."

She approaches me. I can tell that she's off her tits and I pray that I'll hear the shower turn off, that Eddie will again rescue me from the White Devil. Monica runs her fingers through my hair.

"You have nice, hair, Drew. I like guys with long dark hair, like you, Mark and Grant."

"I'm flattered, but I have a girlfriend," I say.

"We could just fool around or something. That's not cheating. Come back here after you drop off Eddie. We can watch Cinemax and make out. Sometimes, that's hotter than fucking. You remind me so much of Mark. We used to fuck all the time until a few years ago. His bitch of an ex-girlfriend Jessica gave him so much grief. I loved being Mark's mistress. It was so hot."

"What was so hot?" says Eddie from the bathroom. I'm hoping he didn't hear anything else.

"I was telling Drew about this party I went to in Malibu where everyone got wasted and skinny dipped," Monica lies.

Eddie walks out of the bathroom. He's shirtless, but, fortunately, wearing jeans. I've seen enough skin for the day.

"Man, I could get used to parties like that," he says. He puts on a T-shirt, not fazed in the slightest that Monica is barely dressed. "I'll be ready in a second, Drew. I just need to hit the head."

When he leaves, Monica kisses me. "I'll be around for a few more hours if you change her mind." She finally puts on her jeans. When Eddie returns she kisses him goodbye, like she's the luckiest girl on the planet.

I take Eddie to Swingers for coffee. He's a wreck. I have a feeling that Mark's going to be pissed off that Eddie's running late. Thankfully, the album's nearly mastered, just one more song to fix. Eddie won't shut up about Monica and the fact that they got cocaine from a guy in the Hollywood Hills.

"Man, she's the kind of girlfriend I've always wanted. She's batshit crazy in the bedroom, and she knows her music, too. She wouldn't drag me down like Karen does to Eric."

No, she'd just cheat on your sorry ass every chance she got. I picture myself pushing Monica's panties to the side as I take her from behind, my hands feeling up her breasts beneath that sexy tank top. I can't get the visual out of my head. The urge to take Monica up on her offer feels as strong as my cravings for alcohol used to be. I try to regain my focus and pay attention to Eddie.

"So, how are things going with Karen and Eric?"

"I don't know, man," says Eddie. "We're doing some out of town gigs this spring to promote the single, like Cleveland, Buffalo, and Chicago, and she's already giving him grief about that."

"Well, you better get your shit together for the U.S. tour when the album comes out."

Eddie seems taken aback, but I'm pissed off. I'm pissed off at Eddie for being a fucking dumbass, pissed off at Karen for fucking with Death Trip's dynamic, and pissed off at myself for lusting after Monica so badly. I'm sober now. I need to stop thinking with my dick like Mark did. I feel let down that he never told me the truth about Monica. He made it sound like they were over years ago. He never mentioned cheating on Jessica. Strangely, the only person I'm not mad at is Monica. Her aim – fucked up as it may be – is true.

The Las Vegas Story

I've always kept secrets from the women in my life. It's not that I've done anything horrible enough to take to the grave – I've never killed a man in Reno – but over the years, I've told my share of fibs. I lied to my mother about drinking when I was in high school because my brother was a total boy scout and I wanted her to think I was a good son, too. When I lived in Dublin with Claire, I used to go to gigs with a female friend named Siobhan. The relationship was platonic, but I didn't want Claire to know that I had a female friend, especially one whose interests mirrored mine so well. With Emily, it was the clandestine post-rehab drinking.

My relationship with Vanessa is different to the ones I've had in the past. I don't get scared or jealous if she mentions a past boyfriend or current male acquaintance. Despite my track record, the thought that she might leave me doesn't enter my mind. And I'm not scared to tell her the truth. I think Vanessa feels the same about me. When I told her details about the Solarstar tour, including my fling with Rose, she didn't bat an eyelid. So, it's a crossroads moment when I come home. Do I tell Vanessa about my sleazy encounter with Monica and her past indiscretions with Mark, or do I keep it to myself? I don't think Mark's going to cheat on Kristi and start doing white lines off Monica's tits, but I feel betrayed by his lie. I tell Vanessa.

"I don't think we should say anything to Kristi, unless it becomes a problem," she says. "But is there anything I should know about you and Monica?"

I pause, remembering how much I lusted for Monica just hours ago but I know it was only a dirty fantasy, that I can keep my dick in my pants.

"No," I say. "I love you to death. It's clear that she's pining for Mark. I remind her of him for some reason."

"Well, you two do have a similar look and style, other than the hair. Hello, Mark, the eighties are over. Ian McCulloch wants his haircut back."

I laugh as Vanessa continues, "If Mark does anything stupid, like sleep with Monica, you have to tell me. Kristi is the only friend who was there for me when I went to rehab. I owe her everything."

The winds calm when Hurricane Eddie leaves town. The Death Trip album is in the can, and the tour dates are confirmed. The first stage will be a west coast stint where the band works their way from Detroit to Seattle, before heading down the coast to L.A. for two gigs. In September, they'll play out east. The Death Trip and Catalina Coast singles have been charting on multiple college radio stations, and Danny has scored a major coup. Catalina Coast have signed to Maverick Records, but because Maverick only wants to release the album on CD and cassette, Danny inks a licensing deal for Cherry Smash to issue the vinyl.

Anton Newcombe has convinced Mark to forge a new direction on his solo album. "Forget about trying to make another Solarstar record," he tells him. "You need to reinvent yourself, like Paul Weller did on *Wild Wood*." The demos I've heard remind me of Johnny Thunders at his most vulnerable, like *You Can't Put Your Arms Around a Memory*. Mark jokes about calling the album *Retox*.

Despite the progress on the recording front, Mark's been aloof. He hasn't been turning up at the office and Kristi has expressed concern that he's pushing himself too hard. Kristi, Vanessa, and I continue with our weekly Runyon Canyon hikes, but Mark rarely joins us. He's either too tired or there's a studio emergency that can't wait.

Mark does attend Vanessa's gallery launch party at a trendy spot hidden behind Hollywood Boulevard. On display is an impressive series of her portraits of punks and goths painted in an Elizabethan style – a mix of the classic and modern. The gallery owner León is a nice guy, a Jean Luc Goddard lookalike with slicked back hair, dressed in a well-tailored black suit and expensive sunglasses. He's not shy when it comes to namedropping; within minutes of meeting him, he regales me with tales of Britney Spears doing cocaine in the green room at a club and Bill Maher's preference for black hookers. Gossip or not, the guy's a hustler and I do spot several celebrities, including Daniel Ash, Vincent Gallo, and Elizabeth Berkley.

Mark seems uncomfortable, so I ask him to join me for a smoke. We step outside and, as if reading my mind, Mark says, "I know I've been a dick, lately. I'm feeling so under the gun with this damn record. I need it to be perfect."

"It's all good, man," I say. "I've been worried about you. We all have. Time is on your side, just get it done at your own pace."

"That's what Anton told me. He played guitar on a few tracks. It's nearly there. I like Anton's attitude. He has this rep for being crazy, but he's prolific. He makes so many great records without overthinking it. I have a hard time letting go. It's been so long since Solarstar. I need to make a statement that Mark Jennings is back."

"I hear you, but don't go all Axl Rose on us."

"It'll be out this year, scout's honor. So, are we good, Drew?"

"We always have been. Pre-seventies men for life."

*

A few weeks later, Kristi and Mark invite us to Las Vegas for a long weekend. We take Kristi's Accord since Mark and Vanessa are both scared that their classic cars might get stolen. Mark is nervous and on edge. About halfway between Barstow and Vegas, he asks Kristi to pull over.

"I feel off. I need to smoke a joint," he says.

We pull over at the next exit. There's a weathered gas station and nothing but miles of desert and cacti in all directions, what U2 once referred to as God's Country. Kristi parks on the side of a dirt road.

"Why don't you join him, Drew," says Kristi.

Mark and I step outside. I look back and catch Kristi whispering something to Vanessa.

Mark takes a long drag and passes the joint to me.

"In case you might be wondering why I'm so nervous, Kristi and I are getting married at the Little White Chapel in a few hours. We want you and Vanessa to be our witnesses."

"Holy shit, Mark. Congratulations."

"Thanks, man. I'm finally doing something right with my life. I'm sober – well, sort of – I have an album coming out, and I'm marrying the love of my life."

As I suspected, Kristi shared the news with Vanessa while Mark and I were getting high. Mark puts *Screamadelica* on the CD player and we soak in the celebratory vibes as we wind our way through the desert into Sin City.

The ceremony is brief and too camp for my tastes. I wince a little as Vanessa and I stand alongside Kristi and Mark, while a boisterous minister, dressed as seventies Elvis, performs the honors. We celebrate with drinks at the Peppermill, an all-night diner with sixties décor. We sit on a circular plush red couch in a sunken fireside lounge. Vanessa tells us that, despite Las Vegas' reputation as a twenty-four-hour party town, the Peppermill is the only establishment open around the clock. The Rat Pack probably haunted it in their heyday, a time when pre-seventies men wore suits, not the ill-fitting baggy shorts and golf shirts found on the Strip these days.

When Vanessa and I are alone in our room at the newly-opened Bellagio, the weirdness of the day sinks in.

"So, you had no idea at all that they were going to elope?" I ask.

"No. Mark's a rock star – they do crap like that all the time – but Kristi is normally so level-headed. She is nuts about him though. Their story is like a Disney movie directed by David Lynch."

"Yeah, crazy Cinderella shit for sure, but I'll take the happy ending."

If Love is the Drug, Then I Want to O.D.

Danny secures an interview with Anton Newcombe for *Left Coast Underground*, the only condition being that he bring Anton a fifth of Maker's Mark. Danny invites me along for the ride. I've been writing reviews for *Left Coast*, nothing extensive like I used to, but it feels nice to tease the creative side of my brain again. Though working at Cherry Smash is fun, much of the daily routine is dull. Movies and television tend to be over-the-top in their depictions of record labels: the gaudy glass and chrome furniture, A&R men in sharp suits ogling smoking hot secretaries, the never-ending *Scarface*-sized white lines. Outside of maybe Death Row, the reality, especially amongst indie labels, is more mundane; processing mail orders, endless calls and emails to writers, chasing up distributors for money to pay artists who badger us for belated royalty checks.

Anton is staying at a friend's apartment, a few blocks away from where Vanessa and I live. Danny parks at our place and we walk to a nearby liquor store to buy bourbon for Anton and a six-pack for Danny. I have a freshly-rolled joint, securely tucked into the inside pocket of my denim jacket.

The apartment where Anton is staying is sparse, just a few pieces of furniture, a small television, and a boombox on the floor placed next to a large stack of CDs. I wish Eddie Zane was with us now, so that he could catch a dose of reality. As prolific and hardworking as Anton has been for close to a decade, he's still a struggling artist. Danny inserts a cassette into his recorder, but Anton isn't in a hurry to get started. He seems distracted. Danny hands him the bottle and Anton walks to the kitchen to open it, returning with the bottle in one hand, a glass in the other.

"You guys really need to see this," he says.

"See what?" Danny asks.

"It's this footage I have of the Manson Family doing campfire songs."

He pops a video into the VCR. Anton's wearing a hippie tunic and beads and I can't help but notice that some of the people we're watching on his TV are dressed the same. Danny cracks open a beer and takes a long gulp, perhaps realizing this interview isn't going anywhere fast. I spark up the joint. After a good half hour of Helter Skelter singalongs, Anton turns off the VCR and plays us some songs from a forthcoming EP called *Zero* and an album entitled *Bravery Repetition and Noise*.

On first listen, the material is great. One track that stands out is a moody piece reminiscent of The Cure, a flat-out love song with real depth, on par with the likes of *The Killing Moon*. Anton tells us that it's called *Open Heart Surgery* because the girl he wrote the song for told him that was how she felt when he first played it for her.

Danny asks about another tune, an up-tempo number with a scuzzy guitar sound and a chorus that repeats the words, "You're so high," before asking "Why can't you fly?"

"It's called '*If Love is the Drug, Then I Want to O.D.*," says Anton.

"Cool title," says Danny.

"I wrote it with Christopher Tucker," says Anton. "You probably know him. He moved here from Philadelphia. He's always at Three Clubs. We were at a party, passing round an acoustic and Christopher started playing something he wrote, and I was like, hey, that's my song! I grabbed the guitar and started playing something I'd been working on. We were using the exact same chord progression."

"I met him once," I say. "He was telling me how much he loved The Jesus and Mary Chain and kept going on about this band he's trying to put together, that we should sign them to Cherry Smash. He's hyper, but in a nice way."

"Whatever," says Anton. "He bailed on me halfway through this recording, so I had to finish the song by myself."

When we finish listening to the tape, Danny begins the interview, asking Anton questions about his less-than-pleasant experience on TVT Records. Anton tells us about the frustrations he experienced; lawyers, producers, the ridiculous costs it takes to put out an album on the macro level. I'm pissed off that here we are, sitting in a small Hollywood apartment, talking to a guy who has released numerous well-received records, yet he's living a bare bones existence. He's defiant though, seemingly immune to those who do not appreciate his vision. He has a rep around town for being a heavy drug user, but he's extremely tuned into to his art. At one point, he tells us that he wants to cover Ride's shoegaze anthem *Vapour Trail* with Miranda Lee Richards on lead vocals because it would be a much better song from the female perspective.

"Those are the words you want to hear from a girl," he says. "Any woman would say, 'That's how I feel.' Any man would go, 'Wow, she's singing about me.'"

When we finish, Anton tells us he'll see us at Three Clubs later. The Warlocks are playing tonight. I've seen them a few times and they're easily one of the best, if not the best, live acts in Los Angeles, a fantastic marriage of The Velvet Underground, Spacemen 3, and an assortment of other dark and evil rock 'n' roll acts.

Danny and I arrive just before midnight. I find Vanessa smoking in the parking lot.

"You're just in time, Drew," says Vanessa.

"For what, the band?"

"Well, that and this."

She slips me an E.

"I just took one. My friend Kelli gave them to me. She's the girl I was telling you about. You know, the one who's obsessed with Corey from The Warlocks."

"Will we be okay with it?" I ask. It's been years since I've done ecstasy and I can't remember much from the experience other than getting silly and wanting to hug strangers.

"It won't make you want to drink, if that's what you're worried about," Vanessa says. "I almost never take it. The last time I took E was at a Chemical Brothers gig in Las Vegas three years ago."

The drug kicks in a few songs into The Warlocks' set, just as they begin their lovely VU-inspired ballad *Song For Nico*. I don't feel overly happy, it's a more clinical buzz, like the stuff was manufactured in a professional lab; twice the strength of a good joint, if you will. I hold Vanessa's hand and gaze at the group from our mid-crowd vantage point. They're all dressed in black, but the singer Bobby is wearing a Mickey Mouse T-shirt. I can't help but smile as I imagine a parallel cartoon universe where Mickey and friends are getting it on to the Happy Mondays at the Hacienda, but most of all, I feel content, like I'm in the right place at the right time. I was lucky enough to experience all the legendary bands like The Stone Roses, The Jesus and Mary Chain, and Primal Scream when I lived abroad but, at times, I felt like I was the proverbial stranger in a strange land. The people in the scene were nice enough to me, but I couldn't help feeling like an outcast, the lone American with similar tastes, but not quite one of the gang.

I bump into Anton when the gig ends.

"You look happy, Drew," he says.

I admit that I took an E.

He snickers and asks, "So, are you higher than the sun?"

Physical Graffiti

Danny and I have been pimping advance copies of the Death Trip album. Rave reviews have rolled in from *Magnet*, *The Big Takeover*, *Spin*, and *Alternative Press*, most comparing the group to The Stooges and MC5, but, more importantly, they're also lumping them in with a burgeoning Detroit garage rock scene. In a case of perfect timing, *Death Trip* is officially released on the same Tuesday in late June as the White Stripes' second album *De Stijl*. The White Stripes are at the forefront of the Detroit rock 'n' roll revival and Danny, Ian and I are more than happy to ride their coattails. Detroit appears poised to become the next Seattle, the latest buzz city in the ever-cyclical nature of music hotspots. Bands from my old stomping grounds haven't seen this much ink since the heyday of The Stooges, MC5 and Alice Cooper.

I've set up interviews with alt weeklies and college radio stations in each of the cities on the Death Trip tour. The press has been great as the band works their way west, though it's worrisome how cocky Eddie has become. He tells a paper in Memphis that he's the best front man since Iggy Pop, commenting that it's only a matter of time before he starts dating supermodels. Danny and I express concern that, perhaps, Eddie is doing too much cocaine, but Ian shrugs it off, saying there's no such thing as bad publicity.

Death Trip roll into Los Angeles on the first Wednesday in July; they'll be playing at Silverlake Lounge tonight with Smallstone and Three Clubs tomorrow. Danny and I greet them at the club and watch the soundcheck. They sound great but it's not hard to pick up on the tension. I'm not the only one who has grown sick of Eddie's shit. The guys in his band are openly calling him 'Eddie Montana.'

When Eddie goes outside to make a phone call, Danny asks, "What's up with *Scarface*?"

"His coke habit is out of control, dude," says Chinaski. "He's acting like he's fucking Axl Rose."

"He fucked a chick in an alley in Portland the other night," says Spence. "Turns out she was the girlfriend of one of the guys in the band who played with us. They got caught in the act and a fistfight ensued. Ugly scene."

"Get him under wraps," says Danny. "Enough of this *Hammer of the Gods* shit."

Chinaski, Eric and Spence shrug their shoulders and look helpless before going outside for a cigarette break – everyone in Death Trip smokes like a chimney. When they're out of earshot, Danny says, "I'm starting to understand why Ian was so hesitant to put out new bands. These guys are morons."

"I hear you, man," I say. "I can kind of deal with the other three, but Eddie is a dick. I liked him when we first met. He was so enthusiastic then."

"Well, he's a fucking cokehead now," says Danny.

"Maybe we can pawn off Death Trip to a major and get some extra cash for Cherry Smash. Do you know what kind of deal they signed with Ian?"

"It was for two albums," says Danny. "Smart move on Ian's part. If the album continues to sell, a larger label might buy the rights off Ian, maybe even reissue the current album."

"It's kind of sad how we just put out their record and we're already looking for ways to get rid of them."

"Maybe it will get better, but this feels like déjà vu, like Ian's going to relive Solarstar all over again."

"When I saw them in Detroit, Eddie was like their puppet master. The other guys were all shy and just dropped in line."

"Looks like we're experiencing a rock 'n' roll version of *Planet of the Apes*, though, to be honest, they're all kind of dumb asses."

I laugh but I have a bad feeling that the first band I've been assigned to work is on the verge of flaming out.

Eric, Chinaski and Spence return.

"Eddie back yet?" asks Eric.

"No," I say.

"He's probably talking to Tripp," says Spence.

"Who's Tripp?" asks Danny.

"He's this skeez-bucket dealer we knew in Detroit. He moved here last year to be a screenwriter. Eddie's probably trying to score."

Sure enough, Eddie returns shortly with a tall, thin dude with long greasy hair; the same guy who was doing coke with Eddie at Three Clubs back in February. Eddie introduces Tripp to me and Danny before asking, "Are you psyched for the show, guys? We're going to tear it up. We're so much better than the last time you saw us."

Silverlake Lounge is a small dark bar and the place fills quickly. The only light is from a neon sign over the tiny stage which says 'Salvation.' The headliners, Smallstone, have a strong following and the *LA Weekly* just published a nice piece by Brendan Mullen, calling Death Trip the first great garage rock band of the new decade.

Vanessa joins me, Danny and Ian near the front. Mark and Kristi decide to bail, saying they'll come out tomorrow. Eddie may be a pain in the ass off stage, but Death Trip still have the goods live, playing a fantastic set, which wins over the Angelinos. They play everything from the album and conclude with an extended version of *No Fun*. "Did we save your souls?" asks Eddie, pointing to the Salvation sign. It's a cheesy gesture, but the crowd laughs and cheers.

I've seen Smallstone several times since Mark first told me about them on the Solarstar tour and they never disappoint. Tonight's show is exceptional. I'm jealous that they signed to Bomp. I'd love to be the one working their new record. The guys are all nice, especially the singer James, whom Danny and I recently interviewed for *Left Coast Underground*.

After the gig, we go to a party at an apartment complex in Silverlake. Most of the people who attended the concert are there, plus a few who weren't, like Anton and some of the other BJM guys. Eddie and Tripp are talking to Monica. Eric's in a corner, making out with a chunky mod chick in a Who T-shirt. It's clear that he doesn't miss Karen, as his right hand slides its way down the back of her low-rise jeans. I take a hit from a joint that's being passed around before going outside for air. The party feels more cramped than the club and I'm experiencing a minor panic attack. I sit on the steps outside the complex and will the summer breeze to calm my nerves.

Monica joins me. She edges close enough to me that I can feel her legs rub against mine.

"Are you okay?" she asks. I haven't talked to her since our Beverly Laurel episode.

"Yeah, just getting some air."

"I was hoping I'd catch you alone. I wanted to apologize for what happened at the hotel. I'm so embarrassed. I was so wasted."

"It's okay," I say.

"Are we good?"

"Yeah."

"Mark's not here, is he?"

"No."

"You probably think I'm psycho for being so obsessed with him, but he was my first boyfriend when I moved to Los Angeles. I thought I was over him. I hadn't seen him for a few years until that night at Three Clubs, and the memories all came back."

"Love sucks, sometimes. You need to get over him."

"I know you're right, but my bond with Mark was like super deep. I did coke for the first time with him. Now he's sober and married, and I'm the one with a broken heart and an expensive habit."

"Have you thought about rehab?"

"Yeah, but I'm scared that my parents will cut me off if I tell them. They think I'm working at Miramax, that I'm living a Hollywood dream life."

She seems sad and broken, a shell of the wild child I had become accustomed to.

"Thanks for listening, Drew. You're a rare commodity in this town."

"How's that?"

"You're nice."

Monica gets up and goes back inside. I think about what she said. It bums me out that not taking advantage of a coked-up girl constitutes being a nice guy in this town. Again, I'm left wondering about Mark. I'd assumed that Monica was at fault, the bad girl who led him astray while he was trying to stay clean. Maybe, it wasn't so black and white.

When I go inside, I run into Vanessa, who is talking to... well, putting up with Eddie.

"Come on, man," he says. "Can't you and Drew take me to South Central? I want to get the *Boyz n the Hood* experience."

"The only experience you'll get is a gunshot to the head," I say.

"Oh, come on dude. We're from Detroit. We're tougher than these L.A. pussies. Don't go faggot on me, Drew."

"Fuck off, Eddie."

I'm ready to fight, but he seems too distracted and wasted.

"Whatever," he slurs. "Monica will take me there, she's cool."

"Good riddance," says Vanessa as Eddie staggers away.

It's early in the morning when Spence and Chinaski say they're tired of partying. The entire band was supposed to crash on our floor until they leave town on Friday, but Eric and Eddie are nowhere to be found.

"Shouldn't we try to find Eric?" asks Vanessa. "I don't give a fuck about Eddie, to be honest."

"I don't give a fuck about Eddie Montana, either," says Chinaski. "He can find his own way home, but Eric will be okay."

"He'll be more than okay," snickers Spence.

"What's that supposed to mean?" Vanessa asks.

"We'll tell you when we get to your place," says Chinaski. "Let's bail."

Skip and Chinaski follow us in their van as we take a straight shot down Sunset, before making a right on McCadden. Vanessa parks the Futura in the lot across the street while I help the guys gather their valuables from the van.

When we get Chinaski and Spence settled in, Vanessa says, "Okay, I'm all ears. What's going on with Eric?"

"He fucked some chick at the party," says Spence.

"Was it that fat mod chick?" I ask. "I saw them making out earlier in the evening."

"Yeah, they were getting hot and heavy when I saw them," laughs Chinaski. "With an emphasis on heavy. It was the same chick. I was walking to the bathroom and I heard some noises inside one of the bedrooms."

"So, you peeped in?" Vanessa asks.

Everyone laughs.

"The door was sort of open," says Chinaski. "I got a nice view of Eric's ass. The chick he was fucking had a big smile on her face."

"Oh, man," I say. "So, did he and Karen break up?"

"No," says Spence, "but she's been giving him a ton of grief. She's calls him like every hour to bitch about something. I don't blame him to be honest."

"They should just break up," says Vanessa.

"You'd think," says Spence, "but Eric has this masochistic streak. He went to Cranbrook. He was groomed for the boring suburban life. His dad's a lawyer. His parents hate him being in a band, and it seems that Karen does, too."

We sleep until the early afternoon. Vanessa gets a pot of coffee going while Spence and Chinaski climb in and out of our living room window, like a pair of monkeys, to smoke cigarettes on the fire escape. A cab rolls up in front of our building and I hear Chinaski yell, "Eric's here!"

We buzz him in.

"Oh man, I fucked up so bad," Eric says when he sits down on our couch. "I don't know what to do!"

He's panicking like he just killed someone or robbed a drug kingpin.

"She had nice tits, though," says Chinaski.

Eric is startled. "You know?"

"Yeah. I saw your skinny ass rocking back and forth."

"You fucking perv."

Spence laughs. Vanessa and I try not to.

"What do I do?" asks Eric. "You're a girl, what should I do, Vanessa? Should I tell Karen?"

"Dude, keep it to yourself," says Chinaski. "Nothing good's going to happen if you tell her."

"I wasn't asking you, dick breath."

"Have you cheated on Karen before?" asks Vanessa.

"No."

"Do you plan to?"

"No. I was just really pissed off at her and was really wasted when I hooked up with that chick last night."

"Then, don't say anything."

"But we're engaged," says Eric. "We're supposed to tell each other everything."

"If you can't keep your dick in your pants for two weeks, you need to keep that to yourself," says Chinaski. "Karen's going to dump your ass if you say anything."

"Tell her when you get home, if you have to," says Vanessa. "It's a dick move to call her from the road."

The Death Trip boys spend the afternoon chain smoking and visiting the assortment of Scientology recruitment centers in the heart of Hollywood to take IQ tests. Eddie phones and says he'll meet us at Three Clubs for soundcheck. I don't ask what he did last night. I'm guessing he didn't go to South Central since he's still alive. We've had enough drama with Eric. The poor guy is pacing around the room and, finally, says he needs a cigarette. He leaves the living room and we hear the front door slam.

"Oh shit, he's going to call Karen," says Chinaski. "Otherwise, he would have just gone to the fire escape."

We gaze out the living room window as Eric, cell phone in hand, paces up and down the sidewalk. When he returns, he's dejected.

"Karen dumped me," he says.

"You're a fucking dumbass," says Spence. "Why didn't you listen to us?"

"I couldn't live with the guilt," says Eric.

"Next time, don't ask for advice so you can go do the opposite," says Vanessa as she rolls her eyes. "Dummy."

The Three Clubs gig isn't a disaster but it's by far the worst of the three Death Trip gigs I've seen. Spence and Chinaski keep the beat, but Eric is out of sync, obviously focused on his break up with Karen. Eddie tries to rattle the crowd when it becomes evident they're not feeling it.

"We're from Detroit," yells Eddie in between songs. "You know, Detroit Rock City. You guys are too fucking mellow. Why don't you go surfing and listen to the fucking Beach Boys if you don't like rock 'n' roll."

There's no after party tonight. If there is, Death Trip weren't invited. Ian and Danny say their goodbyes and head to the Cat & Fiddle.

"Man, that sucked," says Mark. "I wonder if I was that much of a dick when I was on drugs. Was Solarstar that awful when you saw us in Dublin?"

"Close," I tease.

"Eddie needs help, but what's up with Eric? He was on fire when we saw them in Detroit."

I tell Mark about Eric's escapades last night.

"Ah, that explains it. Women and rock 'n' roll is like Mezcal tequila. It's either the high of a lifetime or nothing but bad hallucinations and vomit."

"Speaking of vomit," says Vanessa, "I ran into Tim Burgess in the parking lot. He was like, 'I'd give you a hug, love, but I just vomited in the alley.' His wife was with him. They were pretty wasted."

The entire band crashes at our place after the gig; a miracle of sorts that we're able to wrangle the four of them. They're leaving early for Tucson tomorrow and the mood is far from celebratory. Eddie and Eric are still going at it. Eric is pissed off at Eddie for his onstage banter, while Eddie scolds Eric for letting his extracurricular activities affect his performance.

"Why the fuck did you tell Karen?" says Eddie. "You should never tell your bitch about road pussy. That's rock 'n' roll 101, dude."

"Maybe for you, Eddie, but I take ownership when I fuck up."

"How have I ever fucked up?" asks Eddie. "I'm just having a good time. Read the reviews, dude. Everyone loves us, so get your shit together. Don't bring us down with your negative vibes."

"Fuck you, Eddie Montana."

After the band packs their van and leaves, Vanessa drops me off at work. It's a few minutes past eleven but I'm the first one in. I'm guessing Ian and Danny had a good time at the Cat & Fiddle. The phone rings.

"Hey Drew, it's Monica. Can we talk?"

"Uh, sure," I say, freaked out that she's calling me at the office. Is she stalking *me* now?

"So, what's up?" I ask.

"Eddie beat me up on Wednesday. I was at the ER yesterday."

"Fuck. I wish you would have said something sooner. They just hit the road. I can think of a dozen guys who would like to kick his ass, including his own band."

She feigns a laugh. "I needed time to think. It was a fucked-up situation. We did too much coke and he got violent when he couldn't get it up – sorry, TMI – and he took it out on me. I have bruised ribs and a black eye. I'll survive."

"Crap." I think about Emily and her abusive ex. "You can still press charges. It's not too late."

"I just want to go home. I called my mom and she's checking me into a rehab facility in Louisville. It's back to life with the horsey set."

There's a pause before she asks, "Will you tell Mark I said goodbye?"

She's crying.

"I will."

"Thanks, Drew. Take care of yourself."

When I hang up, I read an email from a journalist in Michigan, who tells me that someone has scrawled 'Eddie Zane hits women' inside one of the ladies' stalls at St. Andrew's Hall.

Live Bullet

It's come to light that Pepsi wants to use the Matthew St. James version of *Bullet* for a UK television advert, namely the "One day I'll die for you" chorus.

"That's fucking disgusting," says Mark. "Matthew has no soul; a love song for a fucking piece of shit soda commercial?"

"They're offering a lot of dosh," says Ian.

"Yeah, just take the money and run," says Danny.

The four of us are having coffee at our favorite spot next door to the office. On today's agenda are marketing plans for Mark's forthcoming album, what to do with Pepsi, and how to keep Eddie Zane from going off the rails.

"I'll think about it," says Mark. "I know Kristi will be pissed if I don't take the money."

"It's not like it's the Solarstar version," I say, "and no one here will even know since it's only going to be run in the UK."

"Speaking of, Mathew is in town next weekend," says Ian. "He's playing at the El Rey Theater. Their management gave me some backstage passes if any of you are interested."

"I'll pass," says Danny.

"I know it's going to suck," I say, "but I'll go. What about you, Mark?"

"Shit, I don't know, man. I guess so. I haven't seen the dude in a good ten years; probably healthy for me to get some closure or kick his ass."

"So, what about Eddie?" asks Danny. "Seems like we need to hire a road manager for the east coast dates to keep them in line."

"How about Sergeant Zack?" asks Ian.

"Who the hell is Sergeant Zack?" I say.

"He's an ex-Special Forces dude," says Danny. "He used to be a minder for some of the hair metal groups on the Strip back in the day. He's still at it. His catch phrase was 'Don't raw dog the road whores!'"

Danny, Ian and I have become engaged in conversation, but Mark has gone quiet. He's put his shades back on, a not so subtle sign that he wants to be left alone.

By Matthew St. James' standards the El Rey is an intimate venue, it's capacity just under one thousand, but it's a lovely art deco building with plush décor, including a private VIP balcony box. It's a perfect setting for a UK million-seller whose sappy over-the-top anthems have yet to win over the American masses.

Ian, Mark, Kristi, Vanessa and I arrive at the VIP box about a half hour before the gig begins. It's like the celebrity guest list was pulled out of someone's ass; an odd selection of models, actresses, indie icon Beck, and old has-beens like Alice Cooper.

"Is that really who I think it is?" I ask Mark, nudging him in Alice's direction.

"Yeah," he says. "He goes to a lot of gigs, actually. He's always looking for hired guns to poach for his touring band."

"You wouldn't think Matthew St. James would be up Alice Cooper's alley."

"He wouldn't be, but a great musician is a great musician. These guys are fucking chameleons; one year they might be touring with a metal band, the next they might be backing a teen idol. It's rock 'n' roll prostitution at his finest."

He has a point. When St. James and his band arrive on stage, they look like they've just returned from an afternoon trip to Fred Segal with their stylist. Matthew is copping a Liam Gallagher look in expensive football hooligan chic, while his lead guitarist is sporting a more expensive version of the Three Clubs look; designer boot-cut jeans and an elaborate western pearl button shirt, unbuttoned halfway down his chest. As a band, they're proficient; the guys know how to play, but something is missing. All the best bands have that 'last gang in town' mentality where, even if they hate each other off stage, there's a certain chemistry and charm to their live performances. The St. James band has none of this; the musicians trying to outdo each other with their showmanship and extended solos, as St. James constantly raises his arms to the sky in full-on Jesus Christ pose.

A string quartet arrives on stage for *Bullet*. The Solarstar original is far more guitar heavy; Mark's acoustic strumming, blending in with St. James' moody power chords. In contrast, the new version unfolding in front of us is like a soulless take on *Bittersweet Symphony*, with its endless orchestral intro and terrace chant chorus. I want to vomit; I can't bring myself to look at Mark.

They leave the stage to a thunderous ovation.

"He could have at least given you some credit," whispers Kristi to Mark.

"That would be too human for him," he retorts.

A security guard leads the VIP entourage downstairs and takes us backstage to mingle with the band. I overhear a girl exclaim, "Matthew is so talented. *Bullet* is like the most beautiful song in the world." I feel like turning around and saying, "Fuck you, bitch. The song is fifteen years old and 'talented' Matthew didn't write it," but I bite my lips.

Due to St. James' longstanding sobriety, the backstage setting is PG-13, nothing visibly stronger than cans of beer and weed on the premises. I can see Matthew from a distance, talking to Beck. St. James is a far cry from the stylish Brian Jones-wannabee rocker he once was, having now morphed into a Lance Armstrong lookalike with his closely cropped blonde hair and toned athletic body. At least he's changed into a tight MC5 T-shirt, though I doubt he's listened to them in years. There isn't an ounce of credibility left in that man.

"I wonder if Beck is trying to convert him to Scientology," says Vanessa.

"Maybe he's just trying to talk some sense into his dumb ass," says Mark. "Beck seems like a cool dude, religion aside."

"We ought to be polite and say hello," says Ian.

We walk over to greet Matthew. When he sees us, he runs over and hugs them both.

"Oh my god," he gushes with clasped hands. "It's so lovely to see you. How long has it been?"

"Too long," says Ian, who seems to be struggling to stay diplomatic.

Mark says nothing.

"So, I hear you have a new record coming out, Mark," says Matthew.

"I do," says Mark. "I think you'll like it. It's got this Johnny Thunders/Only Ones kind of vibe to it... if you're still into that kind of thing."

"Fab," says Matthew as if he were auditioning for a cameo in *Help!*

A young woman approaches with the CD single of *Bullet* in her hand, asking Matthew if he'll sign it for her. I wonder if she's the one I overheard on our way downstairs.

"Of course, love," says Matthew as he signs the cover.

"It's so beautiful," she says. "Thank you so much!"

"Of course, love."

This would have been the perfect time for Matthew to have introduced his fan to Mark and give the real songwriter his due, but I doubt the thought even crossed his mind. Mark's face tenses up. I wouldn't blame him if he lost his guard and punched the smug grin off St. James' face. Matthew's publicist intervenes.

"Sorry to interrupt you honey," she says, "but Vince is about to leave, and he wanted to finalize golf plans for tomorrow."

"Vince," laughs Ian. "What kind of name is that? Are you hanging out with mobsters, Matthew?"

"Uh, no," says Matthew. "Vince is Alice Cooper. We've become good friends over the years."

"So, does Iggy ask you to call him James?" asks Mark.

"I don't know him," says Matthew.

"Just as well," says Mark. "He wouldn't like you."

Matthew appears hurt, but in an instant that false smile returns.

"Gotta run lads," he says.

"He's even more of a cunt now that he's sober," says Mark. "Fuck this shit. I don't know why I bother anymore."

We take a cab home. An old Steely Dan song comes on the radio; you know, the one about the names for all the winners in the world. It pisses me off to no end that Matthew is a 'winner' while Mark struggles with a rock 'n' roll heart of darkness.

The Two of Us

I was saddened when my favorite band The Jesus and Mary Chain split up, so it comes as a pleasant surprise when I learn that Jim Reid and Ben Lurie have formed a new group with Nick and Romi from The Gun Club called Freeheat. We see them perform at the Troubadour. Jim puts us on the guest list; he and Mark have been friends since the eighties when Solarstar shared a few bills with the Mary Chain. It's a nice change of pace from the nightmarish Matthew St. James experience. Mark has been bitching about Matthew non-stop to the point where Vanessa and I have made excuses on several occasions to bail out of plans with him and Kristi. I'm hoping that some time with Jim will help Mark get his mojo back.

Before the gig, we go backstage. I've seen The Jesus and Mary Chain many times, but Jim is one idol I've never spoken to. I try not to appear too star struck when I shake his hand. Jim and Mark go off to a corner to chat while Vanessa, Kristi and I hang out with the rest of the band.

"You looked like you saw a ghost when you shook Jim's hand," says Vanessa.

"I was worried that it would be one of those 'never meet your heroes' moments," I say. "I remember reading a Jesus and Mary Chain interview where Jim said he had an opportunity to meet Lou Reed, but got too nervous and had to pass it up."

"I had a bad experience with Peter Murphy once," says Vanessa.

"No shit?"

"Yeah, my mom and I saw him on the *Love Hysteria* tour when I was seventeen and she pulled some strings, so I could meet him backstage. I was like, 'Very nice to meet you, Mr. Murphy,' and he got all grumpy and said, 'It's Pee-ta,' and stormed off. Maybe I caught him on a bad night, or maybe he slept with a chunky mod girl the night before."

"Rock stars tend to be stunted boys," laughs Kristi, "including the one I'm married to, but he looks so happy with Jim right now. He's been so miserable since we saw Matthew."

Freeheat are loud and great, much better than The Jesus and Mary Chain were on their final tour when Jim walked off the stage in Hollywood only fifteen minutes into their set, one of the final nails in the band's coffin. On the drive home, Mark seems upset. I ask why.

"Didn't you have fun? Freeheat were awesome."

"They were, but that should have been us," he says.

"Who?" asks Kristi.

"Solarstar. I wish we had a career like The Jesus and Mary Chain. They lasted well over a decade and made six great records. We only made one album and as good as it is, we're a footnote. I never wanted to be U2, or, even, The Cure, but reaching a level like the Mary Chain would have been incredible. Jim can do what he wants with the rest of his life. He's a legend, at least to the people who matter. I don't need to sign autographs for airhead models, but a little respect would be nice."

"You still have time," I say. "You can make some awesome solo albums and be the Bowie or Iggy Pop of our generation."

"Maybe, but I feel so fucking old. Christ, I'm thirty-eight. My dad was forty when he died."

"You're not your dad, Mark," says Kristi. "You're sober now. I'll take care of you."

Freeheat have a new EP, which I buy at the gig, called *Don't Worry, Be Happy*. I play it non-stop over the next few weeks. My favorite track is *The Two of Us*, a flat-out love song, where Jim proclaims, "The two of us are getting high. We don't need drugs 'cause we know how to fly.' The song reminds me of my relationship with Vanessa and the redemption Los Angeles has provided me, though I've been slipping in the drugs department.

I've been getting high daily. It's not an around-the-clock habit – just a nightly ritual – but the weed has been giving me messed up dreams. One of them convinces me that it's time for a break. The dream begins in the white space I visited when I tried to kill myself, but, this time, after several minutes of peaceful bliss, I'm greeted by several creatures. Their features are mostly human, but their faces are creepy with exaggerated wrinkles in their skin. They tell me that they've come to take me away, that it's time for me to leave. I plead with them that it's not my time, that I have things to do. One of them grabs me by the wrist and tries to drag me away. I yell and scream until I force myself awake.

Vanessa thinks a short vacation might be the medicine I need. We have lunch with her mom at a restaurant in Beverly Hills with $18 sandwiches and Vanessa asks if it would be okay to borrow her Palm Springs house for a long weekend.

"Vanessa, baby, you do realize it's August. It will be one hundred and fifteen degrees during the daytime. There's a reason I only go there in the winter and spring."

"Drew's never been to Palm Springs. I'll take him to Joshua Tree during the day. It's much cooler in the high desert."

"Suit yourself. So how are you doing, Drew?" asks Suzanne. "Are things getting better with that Detroit band?"

I like Vanessa's mom a lot. She's more interested in my line of work than my own family is, constantly asking me about the ins and outs of the music industry as if she were researching it for one of her novels. Maybe she is?

"Death Trip got home in one piece," I say. "It was their first big tour and, hopefully, the experience will harden them. They were real green when we signed them."

"Eddie Zane's crazy as shit, though," says Vanessa.

"Eddie Zane," repeats Suzanne. "That's quite a name. It's kind of sexy."

"There's nothing sexy about hitting women," says Vanessa.

We drive to Palm Springs on Labor Day weekend. Ian is DJing at a mod club on the Saturday and Vanessa invites Kristi and Mark to join us, hoping that the trip might clear Mark's head, help him get over his St. James-induced blues. Mark's record, which ends up being titled *Retox* after all, will be released in early October and he's been on edge, though the advance press has been fantastic, including rave reviews from *Q*, *Uncut*, and *Mojo*. The latter gave *Retox* a five-star review, snidely commenting that Mark's record should put to rest any doubt on who the real talent was in Solarstar.

"Thanks again for inviting us to Suzanne's place," says Kristi as we approach Palm Springs, racing past an endless sea of wind turbine generators, which look out of place in the otherwise remote desert. "Mark was doing nothing but watching sports last weekend. He was even watching the Little League World Series."

"It's your fault for bringing a TV into my house. I've never owned one until now. Besides, the Little League World Series brings back happy memories. Did you play ball when you were a kid, Drew?"

"Yeah."

"Well, you know how tough it is to make it to Williamsport. Our Bay Village team was one of the best in the country, but we got eliminated in the Ohio Tournament by a team from Tallmadge, who ended up finishing third in the whole world."

"Shit, that's impressive," I say. "None of my teams were that good. I wasn't even a starter."

"Baseball was my game. You were the track star."

"Can you two cool it with sports talk," says Vanessa. "You're starting to sound like a Bruce Springsteen song."

"Amen," says Kristi, who is riding shotgun.

"At least I don't go golfing with fucking Alice Cooper," says Mark.

"Don't you mean Vince," I say.

"You guys," says Kristi. "This weekend is supposed to be fun."

"Sorry," says Mark. "It's just that my life is full of these moments where I almost make it but something beyond my control gets in the way, like Matthew's drug habit or losing that fucking little league game."

We arrive in Palm Springs in the early evening. Suzanne's house is a striking mid-century modern bungalow with a fastidiously manicured lawn and yellow door.

"Christ," says Mark as we enter the front door. "I'm afraid to touch anything. It's like a fucking show home."

"It was owned by a minor forties actress who was married to an oil tycoon," says Vanessa. "The marriage didn't last but she got the house. My mom made some updates, but she's tried hard to keep the original feel."

"It has a pre-seventies man vibe," says Mark. "Speaking of, do you want to smoke before we head out to dinner, Drew?"

I haven't hung out with Mark much since I quit weed, in part because Vanessa and I have avoided him due to his recent severe mood swings, but I'm tempted, not so much because my body is craving it, but because I miss the ritual, the dude time.

"I'm good," I finally say. "I haven't gotten high in a month. I was having some awful dreams, so I took a break."

"That's cool, man," says Mark. "Mind if I step out for a few quick hits, Vanessa?"

"No, that's fine. Let's go to the pool."

Vanessa leads us through the living room to a sliding glass door, which takes us to the pool area. I feel like I'm at a resort as I step on the marbled tile, and gaze at a series of palm trees, which shade the pool.

Vanesa, Kristi and I sit at a canopy-covered table, while Mark walks to the opposite end of the pool, where he straddles the diving board, legs dangling over the water, before toking up. He looks lost and lonely. I feel like I'm betraying him. Vanessa squeezes my hand as if reading my mind.

We drive to Lord Fletcher's, a famous English steak house with adjacent pub done up in over-the-top décor, like a Lord's manor. A large portrait of Winston Churchill greets us as we make our entrance.

"Shit, this place is more English than any restaurant or pub I've been to in England," says Mark.

"The family who own it are expats," says Vanessa. "I imagine Ian would love it here."

"He does," says Mark. "He spends a lot of time in Palm Springs. He keeps saying how he wants to retire here."

"Joshua Tree is great, too," says Vanessa.

"I've never been there," says Mark. "I want to visit the motel where Gram Parsons died."

"That's so morbid," says Kristi.

"Then we'll pretend we're fucking U2 and gaze into the desert and look at cacti. Maybe we'll find whatever the fuck we're supposed to be looking for."

"I was only teasing," says Kristi.

"Fine," says Mark. He's off again, enough so that I wish that Vanessa hadn't invited them along.

"We'll go tomorrow," says Vanessa. "Drew's never been there either. We can go to Pioneertown. That's where they shot a bunch of the old westerns. We'll drive by the Joshua Tree Inn, too. I'll take a picture of you and Drew outside, but we're not going inside. I know someone who spent the night there, and she said the place gave her the creeps."

"Like it was haunted?" I ask.

"Yeah."

Despite Kristi's objections, Vanessa pays for the meal with her Amex Black card.

"You can buy us drinks at the bar," says Vanessa.

"Feels strange to be a kept man," I joke.

"You've kept enough women in your life," says Vanessa. "It's time for someone to watch out for you."

"Doesn't quite go with Mark's pre-seventies man theory, though," says Kristi.

"The concept of the playboy gentleman is as old as time," says Mark, "but, hey, I've started to get some *Bullet* royalties. I certainly don't feel guilty taking money off that cunt. Between that and the fucking Pepsi commercial, I'll be able to pay off the mortgage. I'll get the bar tab."

The four of us spot Ian at the bar with a girl with a Mary Quant haircut wearing a Mondrian dress.

"I wonder if they carded her?" I joke. "She looks young enough to be one of those missing kids on a milk carton."

"Ian's such a predator," says Kristi.

"He's always been that way," says Mark. "He's fifty-five now, but I don't think he's ever slept with anyone older than thirty."

"That's some real *Logan's Run* shit," I say.

"Now, that's a pre-seventies man movie," says Mark.

Mark is perking up. I'm guessing the weed kicked in. Vanessa said that Kristi told her that whenever Mark tries to go more than a few days without smoking, he becomes intolerable. I felt that way for few days when I stopped cold turkey. Vanessa kept calling them 'Mark moods.'

We hang out with Ian and Mary Quant for a few hours. The pub portion of Lord Fletcher's is cozy, reminiscent of some of the older establishments I frequented with my English friends and my expat partner-in-crime Johnny in the eighties. I spoke to Johnny for the first time in several years a few weeks ago, letting him know that I was settled in L.A., that I was living with Vanessa. He hoped that my good luck would rub off on him. He's still in New York and his old band Competition Orange has been playing out again. He said that he and his girlfriend of the past few years split up.

"It's impossible for me to maintain a good rock 'n' roll life and a good love life simultaneously," he said. "It's always one or the other."

When we return to the house Kristi and Mark decide to call it a night. Vanessa and I strip off our clothes and go for a swim. Despite it being after midnight, it's still over ninety degrees and the pool feels warmer.

"Is Mark, okay?" I ask. "I feel like you talk to Kristi more than I talk to Mark these days."

"I think so. Kristi says he's been better since he finished the album. I can tell that he's missed you. Seeing Matthew really upset him."

"I feel so shitty about that. Ian and I thought that they might reconnect or at least find some closure. I've missed Mark, too. He almost never visits us at the office anymore."

"Or Runyon Canyon. Kristi is worried about his health, but he seems okay to me, just tired."

"He'll be okay," I say. "He's not going to tour the new record. Ian's cool with him just playing a few shows around town to promote it. The Solarstar record has given Cherry Smash a second life. Honestly, it's the only thing that's keeping us afloat. The sales have been great. Death Trip are selling okay, too, but Ian gave them a bigger advance than they deserved. I haven't heard any updates from Detroit in a few weeks. I suppose I should phone Chinaski next week. He'll tell me the truth."

"Do you ever miss Michigan?"

"No."

"So, no plans to take me there to meet your mom and dad?"

"I was counting on them coming here."

"I've never seen snow," says Vanessa. "It might be fun to visit them for Christmas or something."

"Maybe. I think my brother's going to visit them this year and introduce them to his new girlfriend. She's a professor, too. Trust me, you don't want to be subjected to that kind of torture. I'm happy in Los Angeles, but I do miss Ireland a lot. Dublin is my favorite city in the world, despite everything that went wrong with my personal life there."

"Would you ever want to live in Europe, Drew?"

"It might be cool, but I do love Los Angeles. I feel like a new person here."

"I get it, but I've been in L.A. forever. I feel pigeonholed as Suzanne Dane's artsy drug addict daughter. Maybe we could pick a place together?"

"What would we do for work?"

Vanessa laughs.

"You keep forgetting that you're dating a rich girl, Drew. We could just go someplace nice where I can paint, and you can write. Life's too short to do things you don't need to do."

I kiss her, and we make love in the shallow end of the pool, before slinking off to our bedroom.

Desert Skies

The four of us have breakfast at a diner before heading to Joshua Tree. Though it's already pushing one hundred degrees, Vanessa tells me to bring my jean jacket. I'm glad I did; it's a good thirty degrees cooler in the mountains. We hit Pioneertown first and walk along the dirt road, checking out the fastidiously constructed film sets, including a bank, motel, general store, and even a bath-house. I wonder how many westerns I've seen with these buildings in the backdrop.

"So, was John Wayne the ultimate pre-seventies man?" asks Kristi.

"I don't think so," I say. "I tend to agree with the *Repo Man* school of thought."

Mark blurts out, "John Wayne was a fag!"

"You guys," says Kristi. I can tell she's happy that Mark's mellow, back to his old self.

"California's such a crazy place," says Mark. "If you play your cards right, you can ski and surf on the same day."

"I love it here, too," says Kristi.

Vanessa and I don't say anything.

"You guys have suddenly gone quiet," says Kristi.

"Drew and I were talking about maybe moving to Europe, not like immediately, but sooner rather than later."

"You can't leave me, Drew," says Mark. "You and Ian are my only real friends."

"It's just something we were thinking about," says Vanessa. "Maybe we'd do something like my mom does where she divides her time between Beverly Hills and Palm Springs. You can't take the California out of me, but I need a break."

Mark and I kill some time in a used record store in Joshua Tree while the girls hit a few vintage clothing shops.

"I like Joshua Tree," I say, "but I bet it gets fucking cold here in the winter."

"You've turned into a pussy, just like me," laughs Mark. "To think we're both from the rust belt where pre-seventies men walked to school in ten feet of snow. Winter in Joshua Tree is nothing compared to Cleveland or Detroit."

"Vanessa asked me if I missed Michigan last night. I told her I didn't. I know her mom well, but she hasn't even met my parents. I think that's eating at her."

"Kristi's mom is visiting from Scarsdale for Thanksgiving. Last time I saw her, I was a punk rock delinquent at Bay Village High School. I'm nervous as shit."

"So, her mom bailed from Ohio, too?"

"Yeah, they didn't like Cleveland. Her dad left NASA and got a research gig at Columbia University, not long after Kristi graduated from college."

"Do you miss New York?"

"Sometimes. It was a crazy period in my life when I was crisscrossing between New York, London, and everywhere else in the world with the Lords. I felt like I was a global citizen. New York has changed so much. It felt so clean when Solarstar played there last year."

"My buddy Johnny got priced out of the lower east side. He's living in Brooklyn now."

"Fucking yuppie developers are ruining everything. You can see it in L.A., too. Silverlake and Los Feliz are fucking expensive."

We grab a late lunch at Crossroads, which is located on the only main road in Joshua Tree, dotted with liquor stores, strip malls, and cacti. We take a quick pit stop at the Joshua Tree Inn where Vanessa snaps some photos of me and Mark. Kristi decides that she wants to get high – normally, she doesn't partake – and Vanessa and I decide to break our fast and join them. It's a beautiful moment. The sun is setting and I'm beginning to feel light-headed as I gaze at the mountains. Maybe it's because I've been off the stuff for a month, but I swear that this Dr. Rock concoction is amongst the strongest blends I've smoked. The girls agree in the affirmative as we make our descent down the windy mountain road into the low desert, an old Pet Shop Boys CD blasting on the stereo.

When we arrive in Palm Springs, Kristi has the munchies big-time, so we go to an old-school hamburger joint to feed her cravings before heading back to the house to rest for Ian's shindig. The guy who is sponsoring the event is an L.A. promoter named Jerry. His mod nights in Hollywood tend to have enforced dress codes, which seems silly to me as Jerry looks like a seventies used-car salesman with his horrible bowl cut and full-blown mustache. He constantly tells his patrons and DJs to "Keep it pure," which apparently includes cocaine. Ian tells me that Jerry deals on the side.

Kristi and Vanessa are wearing sixties-style dresses, but Mark and I decide to test Jerry's limits and dress down. We're both wearing jeans and striped T-shirts.

"You guys look more like rockers than mods," says Vanessa.

"We look like we're in The Velvet Underground," says Mark. "The Velvets are better than any of the pop faggotry that Jerry likes. If he says anything I'll punch that fucking mustache off his face."

"But that's not keeping it pure," laughs Kristi.

I laugh, too. Ever since I told Mark about Ian's 'pop faggotry' outburst at the office, the term has become a regular part of his vocabulary.

The mod night is at the Caliente Tropics Resort; despite the name, it's not so much a resort as a tiki-themed budget motel. Mark and I don't look terribly out of place. A few people are dressed to the nines in sharp suits, but most of the guys are wearing Ben Sherman or Fred Perry without jackets. Summer in Palm Springs is too hot to be fashionable. Ian starts his set soon after we arrive and throws on some floor fillers; obvious classics by The Who, Small Faces, and The Action, plus *Pebbles* and *Nuggets* obscurities that I don't know. He's DJing with nothing but 45s, most of them original first pressings. The crowd is loving it, and even goes nuts when Ian throws on *Communication Breakdown*.

Jerry rushes to the DJ booth and Mark and I follow, knowing something funny is about to ensure.

"You can't play Led Zeppelin," says Jerry.

"Why the fuck not, Jerry?"

"Because they're not mod."

"Jimmy Page was in the fucking Yardbirds, you twat. I can play whatever the fuck I want to."

"Not on my watch. You're not keeping it pure."

"Well, your mustache isn't keeping it pure. You look like a bloody child molester."

"That's it. You're done."

"Done?"

"Yeah. I'm kicking you off the decks."

"Well, fuck that for a game of soldiers."

Ian pulls off the record mid-song and yells to the suddenly quiet room, "This cunt Jerry says I'm not keeping it pure!"

A good number of people laugh as Jerry frantically tracks down another DJ to take over.

Ian packs up his records and joins me, Mark, Vanessa, Kristi and Mary Quant at the bar.

"Well, that was quite the spectacle," laughs Vanessa.

"Fucking cunt, Jerry," mutters Ian. "I need a drink. Should we go somewhere else?"

"I'm really high," says Kristi. "I want to go swimming."

"There's a pool at our hotel," says Mary Quant.

"There's a better one at Vanessa's mom's house," says Kristi.

"Anything to drink there?" asks Ian.

"Full bar," says Vanessa.

"Sold," says Ian.

"Enough of this pop faggotry," laughs Mark.

We smoke some more weed by the pool while the girls undress in front of us and jump into the water.

"Not joining us?" asks Kristi.

"Not me," says Ian. "I'm going to enjoy the show."

"Perv," says Kristi.

Mark is unusually animated, dancing around the pool, like he's Bez from the Happy Mondays, repeatedly singing the chorus to the Pet Shop Boys' *What Have I Done To Deserve This?*

"Fuck if I know," says Ian as if Mark were directing the question to him.

I lay back in my chair and gaze out at the night sky. I'm stoned to the gourd but as high as I am, I can't escape this sneaking suspicion that life can't be this perfect, that this moment is too good to be true.

Crazy Girls

Independent record labels aren't the type of employers who run background checks. Had we done so, we would have discovered that Eddie Zane had several DUIs to his name. He gets a third a few days after we return from Palm Springs, just as Death Trip are about to embark on their east coast tour with Sergeant Zack. Chinaski tells me that in addition to the DUI charge, Eddie got nailed for cocaine possession. A bag of the white stuff fell out of his jacket pocket when he reached inside for his driver's license. Chinaski also says that Eric quit the band, that Karen gave him an ultimatum; it's either me or the band. Eric opted for the former and is filling out law school applications, with Karen gleefully planning the wedding.

"Fucking hell," I say. "So, that's it?"

"Yeah," says Chinaski. "We're done, even if we get a new guitarist, it will be months before we can tour again. I can't deal with Eddie anymore. I just want to rock and have a good time."

When I get off the phone, I tell Danny and Ian the news. Danny shrugs his shoulders like he was expecting it. Ian rips a Death Trip promo poster off the wall and tears it to shreds, just as Mark walks into the office.

"They're not that bad," laughs Mark.

"Maybe that cunt Eddie will OD, and we can sell some records," says Ian.

"Now, that's the spirit," says Danny.

"So, now that you're here, Mark, are you good with playing an acoustic gig at Hotel Café when your album comes out next month? I need to firm up a date."

"Wouldn't Three Clubs be better?" I ask.

"Nah," says Mark with a sniffle. "It's a good scene but it's not my scene, man. I'm an eighties guy. Hotel Café is more my speed."

"Okay there?" asks Ian. "Sounds like you have a cold."

"I'm just fucking beat," says Mark. "That album sucked the life out of me and the Palm Springs trip, as fun as it was, drained me. I need to take it easy."

"I've got the perfect remedy for that," says Ian. "We never did throw you a proper bachelor party."

"Christ," says Mark.

"It'll be fun, man," says Danny. "We'll keep you out of trouble. The album's done, you're happily married. Let's have a dudes' night out."

"What's on the agenda then?" asks Mark.

"I was thinking steaks and strippers," says Ian.

"Just don't take me to Cheetahs," says Mark. "I spent way too much time there in the nineties. I still have an unpaid tab there."

"I prefer Crazy Girls," says Ian.

The next evening the four of us pile into Danny's El Dorado, beginning the night with steaks at the Bounty. Ian and Danny are knocking back Jack and Cokes; Mark seems antsy. Maybe he's craving a joint as much as I am? I have a rollup and ask Mark if he wants to join me outside.

"Nah, I'm good," he says.

That's a first, I think as I walk outside and find a secluded alleyway spot. I take a few hits, hoping it will ease my nerves. I convince myself that nothing's wrong and rejoin the guys inside.

Crazy Girls is packed when we arrive. It's a Thursday night so the A-Team dancers are in full force, shaking their fake tits to overly eager punters who line their G-Strings with bills.

"You do know that they're all lesbians, especially at places like Crazy Girls and Cheetahs," said Vanessa when I told her about our plans.

"I don't think any of us were planning on getting laid," I said. "Except maybe Ian."

"Check out the dancer over there," says Ian. "She's a dead ringer for Juicy Lucy."

"Who the fuck is Juicy Lucy?" laughs Danny as he and I zero in on a brunette with a Joan Jett haircut.

"Oh man," says Mark. "She was this nurse from Liverpool. She and her roommates would always put up Solarstar when we toured there. We called it the whoretel!"

Danny spits out his drink.

"So, if I remember correctly," says Ian, "you and Bobby slept with two of the three. I think Chris was the only one to bag all of them."

"True," says Mark. "I was Juicy Lucy's favorite, but I did fuck Gemma as well. I never got a chance to bag Sharon. She's the one you fucked when they saw us play in London."

"Tasty bird, from what I remember," says Ian.

"Your memory sucks," laughs Mark. "She was on the fat side."

"The bigger the cushion, the better the pushin'..."

"Or, so I've heard," I chime in.

"What about you, Drew?" asks Ian. "Who's the dirtiest bird you've fucked?"

"I suppose it would be this publicist named Rachel, who I picked up at the Columbia Hotel in London back in '95. The sex was kind of vanilla, but she had a gutter mouth."

"Ah, touched by the hand of Blitz," laughs Ian. "I fucked her ten years prior to you."

"Dude, she couldn't have been more then twenty-five when I slept with her."

"To paraphrase Lemmy, if they're able to get backstage, I don't dare ask their age."

"You dirty dog," says Danny.

"What about you, Danny?" asks Mark.

"My last few girlfriends have all been actresses – it doesn't get any crazier than that – but there was this freaky girl I knew in the OC scene in the early eighties. Her name was Hannah. She was obsessed with giving dudes hand jobs. We called them Hannah jobs!"

"Nothing too freaky about a hand job," I say.

"I haven't finished my story," says Danny. "She liked to jerk off guys and have them come all over her tits. Sometimes, she'd take on as many as three or four dudes, or so I heard. I was only on the happy end of a few solo jobs."

"There's a name for that," says Ian. "It's called *bukkake*; quite big in Japan."

"Like Cheap Trick," says Danny.

"Oh, fuck off," laughs Ian, before excusing himself to use the restroom. He returns with the Juicy Lucy lookalike.

"So, who's the lucky guy," she coos. "This lovely Englishman bought a couple of lap dances."

"That would be this lad," says Ian, pointing to Mark.

"You look like someone I should know," says Juicy Lucy.

"Did you ever watch *120 Minutes* in the eighties?" asks Danny. He starts singing *Bullet*.

"I loved that song," she says. "I hate the remake though."

"Good girl," says Mark.

She takes his hand and leads him away.

After a few songs, Ian says, "Fucking hell, I only paid for two dances. I'll take the rest out of his fucking royalties."

Mark is animated when he returns.

"You look well satisfied," says Ian. "What took so long? Did she give you head or something?"

Mark laughs.

"Or a Hannah job," I say.

"Nah, nothing like that," says Mark. "And don't worry, you tight Limey prick; she's only charging you for two dances. We just talked for a while. She told me she had a Solarstar poster on her wall when she was fourteen, man. It made me feel old as fuck, but it's nice to be remembered. So, are we still talking about bukkake?"

"Nah, we've moved on," says Danny, "though I was thinking that maybe Cheap Trick should write a song about bukkake, being that they're both so big in Japan."

"They already have," laughs Mark. "It's called *Cream Police*."

Cocaine Blues

On the weekend following the strip club escapade, I do some record shopping at Aron's. While there, I notice a Death Trip poster on the wall and overhear a guy pontificate about the Detroit scene to his girlfriend.

"Those guys are really good," he says. "Not as good as Outrageous Cherry or The Go, but they're better than The White Stripes."

When I return home, Kristi is on the couch, crying in Vanessa's arms.

"What's wrong?" I ask.

They both look up.

"Don't play dumb, Drew," says Kristi. "I know you think you're protecting Mark, but it's your fucking fault; you and Ian taking him to that strip club."

"I don't have a clue what you're talking about. Yeah, we went to a strip club. Big fucking deal. We had fun. It was all pretty PG-13. It's not like we were doing lines of blow off strippers' tits."

"That's not funny, Drew," says Kristi.

"I'm not trying to be and I'm not protecting Mark. I haven't talked to him since Thursday night."

"I don't think Drew knows," says Vanessa.

"Knows what," I say. "Can we cut to the chase Vanessa?"

Vanessa gives me a stern look. "Do you know anyone named Amber? Please tell me the truth."

"No. Am I supposed to?"

"Kristi found a piece of paper with her name and number in Mark's studio."

Amber must be that fucking stripper, Juicy Lucy. There's no way Mark would stray. It all comes back. How could I be that fucking stupid? The sniffles in the office and at the club. Mark's not cheating, he's using. I'm guessing he did a line or two with Amber after the lap dance. I tell them.

"I think Drew's right," says Vanessa. "Has Mark been acting different since we got back from Palm Springs?"

"He's been livelier, I guess, but he's also been mean and moody."

"He's using again," says Vanessa. "Trust me."

"Where is he now?" I ask Kristi. She's shaking.

"He stormed out of the house yesterday. He's at the Beverly Laurel doing god knows what."

"I'll bring him home," I say.

I feel sick to the stomach when I pull into the motel parking lot. I notice a large dent on Mark's Cadillac. He isn't happy to see me when he greets me at the door. It looks like he hasn't shaved for days, his hair is a greasy mess, and his eyes are bloodshot. There's a Dodgers game blasting in the background.

"What the fuck do you want?" he asks before reluctantly letting me in. He takes a seat on the edge of the bed, while I pull out the desk chair and sit opposite him.

"Come on, man," I say. "Get your shit together, Mark. What the fuck is wrong with you? Kristi is worried sick."

"Like she gives a fuck. She thinks I'm cheating on her. It's your fucking fault; you, Ian and Danny."

"It's our fault that you got a stripper's phone number? Tell me the fucking truth. Are you fucking her? I won't tell Kristi or Vanessa if you made a mistake."

"So, you don't believe me either, Drew? After all we went through together."

"I don't know what to believe, except the obvious."

"And what would that be, Sherlock?"

"You're using again. Let me take you home."

"Fuck off, man. Leave me alone."

"I'll leave if you tell me the truth."

"Okay asshole, I did a bump in Palm Springs at that mod club and I did a line with Juicy Lucy. She gave me her number in case I wanted more. I never called her back. Happy now?"

"No, but I believe you."

I don't believe him. I'm guessing Mark's been doing blow all weekend by the looks of him, but all I'm focused on now is getting him home, getting him the help he needs.

"Then just leave me alone. I need to clean up. I don't want Kristi to see me like this. I'll call her tomorrow."

"She wants to see you now. She's worried sick. Please, man. You'll kick this motherfucker like your old team should have done to Tallmadge."

"You dick, trying to guilt me with a pre-seventies man sports story."

He breaks down and cries. I sit next to him and hold him.

"It's going to be okay," I say. "Just a little relapse."

"It's all too much," he says. "Fucking Matthew St. James. It breaks my heart that I mean nothing to him now. My fucking album sucked the life out of me and no one even cares. I have nothing left. I'm so fucking exhausted."

"You don't have to do anything, except get healthy."

Mark showers and shaves before I take him home. I reassure him that we'll collect his car in the morning.

Brother, Can You Hear My Voice?

The next morning Vanessa phones me at the office in a frenzied state. She can barely compose herself as she tells me that Kristi's mom is boarding a plane to Los Angeles. Mark passed away in the early morning hours at Hollywood Hospital. From what Vanessa can gather, he collapsed on the couch, just a few hours after I dropped him off. The medics rushed him to the hospital but were unable to revive him. The doctors said that Kristi is in a severe state of shock. Vanessa's on her way to the hospital to comfort her. I tell her we're on our way.

I start bawling when I hang up.

"What's wrong, mate?" asks Ian.

"It's Mark. He's dead."

Danny and Ian start crying, too, the three of us awkwardly hugging each other.

We gun it to the hospital and find Vanessa in the waiting room. She was able to speak to a doctor, who told her that Mark suffered from a heart condition called mitral valve regurgitation. In layman's terms, Mark had leaky valves, which enlarged his heart to the point where it just stopped working. Traces of cocaine were found in his system, which more than likely pushed him over the edge.

"Fuck," says Ian. "He seemed tired all summer, but I thought it was because he had been pushing himself so bloody hard on the album."

"Kristi kept bugging him to get a physical," says Vanessa. "She's going to blame herself."

"Did you know he was using again, Drew?" asks Ian.

"I didn't figure it out until yesterday. Kristi was going to take him to the doctor today. Apparently, he did a line with someone asshole at that mod night in Palm Springs and some more with that stripper at Crazy Girls."

Ian pounds his fist on a table.

"It had to have been that cunt Jerry. I'm going to kill the fucker. Mark my words."

He breaks down in tears and buries his head into his knees, while I hold Vanessa. Danny is composed enough to bring us coffee.

*

Several weeks later, we hold a wake at the Cat & Fiddle, scattering Mark's ashes in the courtyard. Many people turn out, including Matthew St. James, who flies in from London. No one is happy to see him, though I do get a kick watching him squirm when the DJ plays the original version of *Bullet*.

Kristi returns to New York. Vanessa and I move to her mother's guest-house in Beverly Hills. Work has become more like group therapy than a job as Ian, Danny and I spend countless hours talking about Mark. Sometimes, it feels like he's still with us; that he could walk into the door any minute. Mark's album is released on schedule and is well received, though I'm saddened that he's on the path to becoming what he feared most; famous when dead, a tragic figure like Ian Curtis and his beloved friend Stiv Bators.

Vanessa and I get married in the spring, just a simple ceremony with family and friends at the Ritz-

Carlton in Laguna Nigel, which overlooks the ocean. Vanessa wanted Kristi to be her maid of honor, but Kristi declined, saying that she wasn't ready to return to California.

We decide to honeymoon in Marrakech, which borders the Sahara Desert. Before we leave, I finally go through several boxes of Mark's records that Kristi left behind for me. I notice a pattern; every single one of them has Mark's initials scrawled in black ballpoint on the bottom right hand corner of the back sleeve.

"I didn't realize he was so OCD," I tell Vanessa.

"It's not that," she says. "It was his way of making sure no one took them from him; he had abandonment issues. He lost his dad, his mom went crazy, Kristi got sent to boarding school, and Matthew broke his heart. I can't believe that asshole showed up at the wake, like it was a bullshit PR stunt."

"I wish I could have done more for Mark. I should have seen the signs."

"You did. You had no way of knowing about his heart condition, and you need to watch yours. I know it's just a murmur but I'm not going to let you die on me."

She cries. I hold her tight, until she composes herself.

*

We arrive in Marrakech, just before sundown, jet lagged from a day's worth of traveling; L.A. to New York, New York to Amsterdam; Amsterdam to Marrakech. My hair's greasy and I haven't shaved in a few days, but I catch a second wind as we walk off the plane Beatles-style on a moveable ladder. We're escorted to the airport by armed security. I haven't witnessed this much military presence since I visited Belfast during the height of the Irish Troubles.

The cab journey to the city feels like an amusement park ride as our driver weaves through traffic with seemingly no regard for human life, dodging numerous scooters and motorbikes, some of them driven by women with toddlers on their laps. We arrive at the main square where we are greeted by a gentleman from our hotel. He places our luggage in a wheelbarrow and Vanessa and I follow him in hot pursuit as he weaves his way through a series of alleys, often interrupted by mopeds, which zoom past us with zero warning. The scenery is enchanting, the moon and stars giving the buildings a golden glow. Several young men offer us hash; maybe they think we're descendants of Keith Richards and Anita Pallenberg. I'm tempted, but Vanessa nudges me forward, urging me to keep up with our speed racer attendant.

Our hotel is deep in the heart of the centuries-old city. It's a modest riad, which was once a military fortress. When we settle in, we fall into a daily routine. In the mornings, we have breakfast on a rooftop where we are often visited by alley cats, who leap from roof to roof. There's a black cat, who often sits on my lap. During the day, we visit cafes and shop in the sooks, where Vanessa barters for cheap jewelry with overly-persistent merchants. In the evenings we sit and sip mint tea in the flat-roofed courtyard next to a large tree, not quite believing we're so far away from Los Angeles.

The distance is helping me heal. It still hurts every time I think about Mark but being in his favorite city makes me feel like I'm bonding with him from beyond the grave. I remember how he buzzed with excitement when he told me about Morocco when we were in rehab, and this makes me smile.

"I think Marrakech is the best place I have ever visited," I tell Vanessa one morning, as we listen to the echo of calls to prayer from the rooftop.

"Same here," she says. "You look happy again. I was waiting for the right moment to tell you this."

I freeze.

"It's nothing bad," she says. "Just closure. Before she left Los Angeles, Kristi gave me the rest of Mark's ashes. She asked me if you would scatter them for Mark if we ever visited Morocco."

I begin to cry. She holds me.

"I know where," I say.

We walk down several flights of stairs to the courtyard and I point to a large tree.

"Mark told me that he wanted to grow old in Marrakech and spend his days in a courtyard like this, where he could drink mint tea and listen to records."

Vanessa removes a small jar of concealer from her purse.

"I hid them inside."

I scatter Mark's ashes into the dirt, thinking about the day we met in rehab, how we talked about The Chameleons. The chorus from *Intrigue in Tangiers* rings in my ears: "Brother, can you hear my voice? Brother, can you hear my voice? Every second that you cling to life you have to feel alive."

I break down in tears and collapse. Vanessa is there to catch my fall.

If you enjoyed this title, follow Obliterati Press on
Twitter and Facebook for details of forthcoming
releases.

@ObliteratiPress

https://www.facebook.com/ObliteratiPress

Also, be sure to check out our website for regular
short story contributions.

Also available from Obliterati Press:

LORD OF THE DEAD

Richard Rippon

A woman's body has been found on the moors of Northumberland, brutally murdered and dismembered. Northumbria police enlist the help of unconventional psychologist Jon Atherton, a decision complicated by his personal history with lead investigator Detective Sergeant Kate Prejean.

As Christmas approaches and pressure mounts on the force, Prejean and Atherton's personal lives begin to unravel as they find themselves the focus of media attention, and that of the killer known only as Son Of Geb.

Also available from Obliterati Press:

THE BAGGAGE CAROUSEL

David Olner

Dan Roberts has a troubled past, anger management issues and a backpack named after an abducted heiress. A chance encounter with Amber, a free-spirited Australian girl, seems to give his solitary, nomadic life a new sense of direction. But when she doesn't respond to his emails, the only direction he's heading is down…

'The Baggage Carousel' is a visceral yet humane travelogue of a novel about life's great let-downs; family, work and love. Dan Roberts is destined to go down as one of fiction's great solitary men, equal parts Iain Banks' Frank, Camus' Meursault and Seuss' The Grinch.

Also available from Obliterati Press:

WE KNOW WHAT WE ARE

Russ Litten

We Know What We Are is the debut short story collection from novelist Russ Litten, author of *Scream If You Want To Go Faster, Swear Down* and *Kingdom*.

This batch of tense and edgy tales are all centered in and around Hull in the year 2017 and feature a cast of citizens whose lives play out in the furthest edges of the City of Culture spotlight.